You're the best and
we should know.

Merry Christmas
We love you,
Your Girls!
2000

Walls Rise Up

WALLS RISE UP

George Sessions Perry

with a foreword by Judyth Rigler

Texas Christian University Press/Fort Worth

Walls Rise Up is Number 21
in the Texas Tradition Series.
James Ward Lee, series editor.

Foreword copyright © 1994, Texas Christian University
First published by Doubleday Doran in 1939

Library of Congress Cataloging-in-Publication Data

Perry, George Sessions, 1910–1956.
    Walls rise up : a novel / by Geroge Sessions Perry ; with a fore-
word by Judyth Rigler.
        p. cm. — (The Texas Tradition Series ; no. 21)
    ISBN 0–87565–126–7
    1. Tramps — Texas — Fiction. I. Title. II. Series
PS3531.E687W35   1994
813'.52 — dc20   93–37785
                                                                    CIP

The chapter title decoration is based on a piece of hobo graf-
fito that means "go" or "this is a good road to follow." The
TCU Press staff thanks artist and professor David Conn for
guidance in the use of such symbols.
    The cover photo is courtesy of the Environmental Section,
Texas Department of Transportation.

The dust jacket and text for *Walls Rise Up* were designed by
Barbara Whitehead.

Foreword

George Sessions Perry (1910-1956) is perhaps best remembered for his 1941 novel, *Hold Autumn in Your Hand*, the first book ever to be given the National Book Award. (In 1945, it was made into the movie *The Southerner*.) The Rockdale, Texas-born writer became a respected war correspondent and produced magazine fiction and nonfiction and a variety of books: *Texas: A World in Itself* (1942), *Roundup Time* (1943), *Hackberry Cavalier* (1944), *Where Away* with Isabel Leighton (1944), *Cities of America* (1947), *Families of America* (1949), *My Granny Van* (1949), *Tale of a Foolish Farmer* (1951), *The Story of Texas A&M* (1951) and *The Story of Texas* (1956).

Perry's first published novel, *Walls Rise Up*, was released in 1939 by Doubleday Doran. Like many if not most first novels, *Walls Rise Up* came only after an eight-year apprenticeship during which Perry wrote half a dozen novels that no one would publish. There were also dozens of unpublished short stories produced during those years, according to Maxine Cousins Hairston's 1973 biography, *George Sessions Perry: His Life and Works*. But from 1937 to 1939, Perry's stories began appearing in *Saturday Evening Post*, *Esquire*, and *Cosmopolitan* magazines, and his seemed a marketing success story from that point onward.

While most critics have mentioned Perry's debt to the inspiration of John Steinbeck's work (*Hold Autumn in Your Hand* is invariably linked to *Grapes of Wrath*, and *Walls Rise Up* to Steinbeck's comic novel, *Tortilla Flat*) success of the small novel *Walls Rise Up* surely must be linked to the spirit of abandonment and joy in which it was written.

"I love this book," Perry said of *Walls* upon its 1945 republication. "I wrote it when I was young. In it there are errors of taste and judgement which, alas, I will never make again. If the reader has half as much fun reading this book as I did writing it, I certainly, and I hope he, will have been repaid."

Hairston writes that Perry took his inspiration for the book about three Depression-era boxcar tramps who spend a summer camping out under a Brazos River bridge from a train trip he had taken. He wrote *Walls* quickly, and his wife Claire is quoted on the process in Hairston's book: "We had more fun with [*Walls Rise Up*] than anything else he had ever written. Each morning he got out the writing board . . . wrote a chapter or two, then yelled for me. He read me what he had written and we were always convulsed by it."

One could scarcely find a book that is more politically incorrect than *Walls Rise Up*. Yet the reader, more than half a century later, finds it easy to laugh at descriptions of shiftless hoboes, alcoholics, loose women, dimwitted giants, liars, thieves and the like. (Today, we'd call them vocationally undeserved, libationally overindulgent, sexually indiscriminatory, mentally challenged, veracitorily inconsistent, or morally dysfunctional.)

Perry's editor for *Walls Rise Up*, Harrison Smith, reported in his preface to the 1945 reissue that the Depression and the thousands of young men who took to the rails in search of a new start spawned a number of novels before Perry's. "It had become one of the minor themes of that gloomy symphony of self-conscious proletarian literature to which we had to listen for several years, and to which the American reading public had turned a deaf ear; or rather had let it go into one ear and out the other without anything noticeable happening between. The W.P.A. [Workers' Progress Administration] Writers' Project was responsible for many of these dreary books on how repulsive life could be in America, but there were plenty of writers who needed no stimulus from the government's seventeen-fifty a week to be as depressing as possible, or of critics who hewed close to the party line and who demanded that novels have 'social significance,' whether the public liked it or not."

Perry's little novel was different, and the public did like it — although it received little attention before it was reissued in a 115,000-copy paperback Armed Services edition in 1944. The author didn't dwell on the downside of life in the 1930s. Instead, he let

Jimmy, Mike, and Eddie revel in their freedom from work schedules, responsibilities, and the restrictions of society in general. He let them drink themselves into dreamless slumber at night and wake refreshed to another day of taking whatever life provided (even when it belonged to someone else) and be grateful for it.

Part of the reason it is possible to forget that these men represent the dregs of society is that Perry manages to elevate his hoboes, allowing them to speak in terms of larger concepts than survival and to put just the slightest twist on ideas and beliefs we hold dear. Something so seemingly harmless as choosing a destination comes under the heading of taking too much control, according to the threesome's philosophical advisor, Jimmy. When Mike and Eddie begin contemplating whether they'd be better off to take a boxcar into Minnesota or Delaware, Jimmy says, "That's the trouble with you boys. You're always trying to force the hand of Providence. Why the hell don't you just relax and go where the Higher Powers aim for you to go?"

So they do, trusting in those Higher Powers to show them a sign, and the reader is treated to a rollicking, ribald adventure that surely must have lifted the spirits and lightened the steps of all who read it in 1939. It's escape fiction at its best, and one can't afford to analyze it too seriously. There's hardly time to, anyway, what with all the brawls, con jobs, out-and-out thefts, beer drinking, and woman chasing.

It is worthwhile, however, to take a look at what makes the book flow so effortlessly, besides all the action that's packed into the slim volume. For one thing, Perry is the master of understatement; following a night in town with three ladies who "didn't hold their favors at any king's ransom," they hop aboard a daylight freight because Jimmy still has not seen a sign. Eddie, the narrator, observes: "Mike, who always got to say something, said we'd all probably be seeing certain signs in eight or nine days."

Perry's episodic structure holds the philosophizing and wisecracking together. When the trio happens upon the fishing camp of a hobo hit by their train ("he contested that fast freight train for the right of way," in Jimmy's words), they discover that it has everything they could possibly want — including plenty of catfish already on trotlines, thanks to the labors of the hapless Sam. They feel bad momentarily about poor Sam and know that the dead hobo could just as easily have been any one of them, but Jimmy can be counted on to put a good face on the tragedy. ". . . it goes to prove what I always said. . . . Everything turns out for the best if you get there in time."

Later Jimmy waxes even more philosophical: "Walls rise up out of the earth to protect the pure in heart. At times, when it was necessary, light bread has been known to fall out of the sky." Who could fail to appreciate such wisdom, based as it is on Jimmy's brand of biblical interpretation? Certainly not Mike and Eddie, who aspire only to be as wise as their elder and are willing to work hard to ensure that the weaker Jimmy isn't physically taxed, even when he seems to be pushing his luck a bit. The respect with which Mike and Eddie treat Jimmy, a shiftless alcoholic and con man with a gift for gab, is strangely endearing and helps to establish their characters — and Jimmy's — in the reader's mind.

Almost every paragraph of *Walls Rise Up* holds a good laugh and an affirmation of character in its fullest sense — that combination of eccentricities that makes a person memorable. Getting established in their new home, the three are surprised at the bounty within their reach. When they look up on the river bank and see a woman herding turkeys, Jimmy notes that they should pick up a nickel's worth of garlic at the store; the dressing will taste flat without it. On another bank is a truck farm. Jimmy won't believe it's anything more than a mirage; Mike and Eddie try to convince him, but finally there's nothing for it but to pick a bucket of mixed vegetables to bring back to the incredulous Jimmy. And they have so many catfish that they strike a deal to trade the excess at the store for beer — but not before tricking the hated storekeeper, Newt, out of a massive quantity of food and beer, to say nothing of his wife's favors.

Another element that lifts the story above pure escapist adventure is Perry's description of the natural world, as seen through the eyes of the simple-minded but sometimes eloquent adventurers. After an evening spent drinking beer and eating cheese and baloney at Newt's, Eddie and his pals head up the road to their humble home. "It was a nice clear night. The south breeze was blowing and the moon was coming up big and orange over on the other side of the truck farm. It was really wonderful walking down that road full of beer to your own camp." It's such a fine night, in fact, that they decide to go fishing. Just before dawn, Eddie observes, "It was nice, all right, there on that sand bar with the sky turning gray up above the east bank. You know how still it can get a lot of times right at dawn. The river was just like a piece of slick gray glass." And who can forget the island, "long and sort of curving, about the shape of a raw weenie. . . ."?

Whether Perry wrote *Walls Rise Up* as a reaction to a society grown moribund with puritanical thinking and a mindless devotion to the work ethic, or simply as a carefree adventure about three lovable ne'er-do-wells who are more boys than men, the book has held up remarkably well. A model for those studying economy of character, plot, and humor, *Walls Rise Up* is a unique and satisfying picaresque novel that deserves to be read for years to come.

Although Perry's novel might not find favor with today's editors and critics because of its unstylish world view, the original manuscript was far more risque in that regard than the finished product. Maxine Hairston notes in her biography that the first draft "carried satire of conventional ethics beyond what appeared in the final version." A 1000-word section that originally came at the end of Chapter 7, in which a priest visits the camp and spends an afternoon drinking with the boys, hearing "detailed" confessions of their sins and then preaching a profane mass, was deleted at the request of Perry's editor, Jim Poling. Hairston quotes Poling: "It has always been our experience that taking cracks at the Catholic Church, while perhaps we may feel it is justifiable in the story, is dynamite in a book."

Perhaps it was this same squeamishness that led to the deletion of another missing chapter that is included at the end of this reprint, although no verification of editorial censoring exists in Hairston's biography or other sources. When a rise in one of the rivers running into the Brazos creates a mini- flood that brings a church floating around the bend one Saturday morning, the boys are aghast, especially when the church lands "smack dab up" on Weenie Island. They decide that this miracle deserves recognition, and a Sunday morning service at the newly ordained Weenie Island Church, with Jimmie preaching his curious brand of religion and Oof putting in his two cents' worth, is described in hilarious detail.

Blasphemous or not, the chapter has been deemed most worthy of inclusion in this reissued version of *Walls Rise Up.*

(The original of the missing chapter, along with more of George Sessions Perry's personal papers and unpublished materials, is on file at the Harry Ransom Humanities Research Center at the University of Texas at Austin.)

— Judyth Rigler

Walls Rise Up

Chapter One

I knocked on the door then stepped aside so Mike could do the talking.

We heard some soft, heavy steps coming and I knew it was a fat woman in bedroom slippers. When she got there she looked at us and said, "Yes?"

"I hope we didn't disturb you," Mike said, "but we have a little friend who needs a coat. You know how this California night air is. We thought if you had an old one. . . ."

"Honest," I said, "it's not for us. We're big. All we're asking you for is a little one."

We saw she was thinking. At least she was not going to say no straight out.

"If I'm not mistaken," she said, "we've still got that old plaid coat Barney used to wear when he worked out at Paramount. Just take a seat and I'll go see."

We played with the cat while she was gone.

"Well, here it is," she said when she came back. "I hope he can get some good out of it. That hole in the pocket is where I tried to take out a stain."

We said it was all right about the hole and thanked her.

She reached in her pocket and pulled out a half dollar.

"Maybe this would be some help," she said.

I don't know why but fat women are nearly always the most generous.

We thanked her and God-blessed her and left, walking down the street thinking about that half dollar.

"He's out of razor blades," I said.

"Of course," Mike said. "And tobacco too. Ain't he always out when we get hold of a little money?"

"I'm glad we had his shoes half-soled last week," I said.

"He's an expense," Mike said, "but what worthwhile ain't?"

"I guess so," I said and laughed.

Mike laughed too. It's enough to make anybody feel good to have presents for Jimmy.

We bought Jimmy's stuff and went on back up to Melrose and Vine where he was sitting on one of those orange bus-waiting benches.

He was just sitting there with his hat on the bench sunning his bald spot and holding that old crooked walking stick across his knee, enjoying the weather and, I guess, life, and watching those funny people pass.

Mike handed him the coat.

Jimmy's eyeballs bugged out nearly as far as his forehead.

"For me?" he says.

"Yes," I says, "it's all yours."

He took it out of Mike's hand and went all over it, feeling the material and rubbing it on his face to prove it was wool. He was awful careful to keep from noticing the hole.

"Boys," he says, "if this was over in Egypt back in Bible times, my life wouldn't be worth a copper cent. They would beat me up like they did Joseph and run off with my coat. For I'm sure," he says, "little Joe's hadn't half the good wool this one's got nor was nowhere near so loud."

"I want to see the color of anybody's eyes that takes that one away from you," Mike said.

"Just let 'em try," I said.

He put it on and it looked wonderful. The shoulders were a little roomy but they had plenty of good stiff padding in them so it really didn't show.

We gave him his blades and tobacco and admitted having thirty cents left.

"Maybe we ought to get some baloney and bread," Mike says.

"They've got beer over at that store for a nickel a bottle, ice-cold," Jimmy says. "That's two bottles apiece and, if it's anything more than rain water, it ought to help us."

"O.K.," Mike says. "Only we haven't had anything to eat today besides that puffed can of spinach."

Jimmy said the United States government would take care of that.

We said all right and went over to the store and drank six bottles of beer. Then we went downtown to the relief station.

But when we got there the man said nothing doing.

"How come?" Mike said.

"Because you haven't lived here six months."

"You can't prove we wasn't here," Mike said.

"Besides," the man says, "if you've got any relatives that own a house in any other state, you're their responsibility, not ours."

"Well, all I can say," Mike says, "is that's about the shortest thing I ever heard of."

"I just wish you knew our kinfolks," I said. "They can't hardly take care of theirselves, let alone us."

"There's no use to argue," the man said. "You just heard the rule."

"To hell with the rule," Mike said; "we was counting on getting supper here."

"Never mind," Jimmy says. "If they don't want us out here, we'll go somewheres else."

"No," Mike says, getting mad, "we ought not to let them get away with a thing like this."

"I think we better take a little trip," Jimmy says. "I'm kind of lonesome to get back to civilization."

"How was that?" the man says.

Mike turned and told him what he could do with California.

"And if there's any room left," Mike said, "you can do the same with Catalina Island."

We started down to the L.A. freight yards.

On the way we picked some fruit off of some trees and Mike was able to borrow a dime here and there from people on the streets. We bought some baloney and bread and the man threw in an onion, though he wasn't very crazy about doing it.

A block from the tracks, Jimmy noticed a parked delivery truck with five-gallon bottles of Shasta water in the back. He began to discuss the heat and dryness and size of the desert.

Naturally he didn't come out with an open suggestion. Jimmy is never crude. But those bottles are heavy and unwieldy, and me and Mike just kept walking.

But when Jimmy began to get quiet we couldn't stand it, and Mike said, "All right, Eddie, let's go back and get Jimmy's water."

We loaded our stuff into a boxcar and started eating.

"Where you reckon we better go?" Mike says.

"I never have been to Delaware," I said.

Mike said he'd always heard Minnesota was mighty cool and pretty.

"That's the trouble with you boys," Jimmy said. "You're always trying to force the hand of Providence. Why the hell don't you just relax and go where the Higher Powers aim for you to go?"

We talked a lot about that.

Mike said aimlessness was bad for people.

But Jimmy said, "There's a place on this earth for every last stinking one of God's creatures. When you're in the right place," he said, "you're in harmony with everything around you. There's a spring in your foot and groceries in your belly. Otherwise, it's just one damn thing after another. And who's to say our place is in Delaware or Minnesota?"

"Who's to say it ain't?" Mike said.

"I'm not saying it ain't," Jimmy says. "I'm just saying that if it is, and we ride enough freight trains, the Higher Powers will drift us there. . . . I just said it's wrong and pigheaded to have any picked-out place. And for my part, I ain't going to none."

Finally Mike said all right.

"I guess I'm ignorant," I said to Jimmy, "but will these Higher Powers let us know when we get there?"

"We'll get the word," Jimmy said, "or a sign or something."

"Ain't signs a little out of date?" I said.

"A lot of folks thought that back in Holy Grail times," Jimmy said, "but the pure in heart have always seen 'em and I guess we stand as good a chance as those Grail hunters."

Mike wanted to know what a Grail hunter was but it turned out to be over his head.

Then the engineer gave a couple of toots and hit that string of boxcars and jerked them rolling.

We did all right until we got about halfway through New Mexico. The train stopped and our door swung open.

A man in a big hat with a flashlight in his hand said, "All right, boys, hit the ground."

"For what?" Mike said.

"We got the God-awfullest crop of lettuce here you ever saw and looks like it all needs cutting at once."

"Well, what's that to us?" Mike said.

"Nothing except you're gonna cut it. You get a dollar a day and board."

"I thought this was a free country," Mike says.

"No," the constable says, "you thought everything in it was free. But by God you're gonna cut lettuce for the next couple of weeks or go to jail."

"All right," Mike said, "you got us. Me and Eddie'll

cut. But our friend here would never be able to stand up to it."

"Lettuce ain't heavy."

"And neither is Jimmy," I said. "Do you want to kill him?"

"Never mind, boys," Jimmy said. "We will make out all right with this constable. I can tell he is a fair, intelligent man just trying to do his honest duty. After all, a constable is not supposed to be a doctor."

Now we were at the car. What Jimmy said had not altogether broken that Law down. Just the same he held the front door open for Jimmy and said for Mike and me to get in the back.

It was a couple of miles to town from the depot.

"Where you boys from?"

"Hollywood," Jimmy said.

"Ever see old Tom Mix out there?"

"Sure. You a fan of his too?"

The constable said he was.

"He drives around Hollywood a lot in an old Cadillac and a big hat."

"He's sure good," the constable said.

"I got a couple of his autographed pictures at home back in Kentucky," Jimmy said. "I guess I could write the folks to send me one out here."

"Be pretty nice tacked up over my desk," the constable said."

And it went on from there.

Finally Jimmy told him that one about the eleven acres of wheat field that got flattened in such a curious way and that nearly killed him. So we didn't worry any more. We knew Jimmy would never cut any lettuce.

7

After a couple of weeks they said we could go. We went into town and met Jimmy down at the constable's office where he was rooming.

"How about it?" I said. "Do you want to go on? Or have the Higher Powers give you a sign to stay?"

"Boys," he says, "I've looked hard everywhere but this place is as bare of signs as a dog's behind is bare of honey."

So we caught a train and got into San Antonio about sundown the next day.

We left the train at that chili factory and made straight for Jesus Garcia's joint, where we ate some enchiladas and drank seven dollars worth of beer. That left us with a dollar apiece and a little change and Mike suggested we take a stroll down into a certain part of town.

When we got there we agreed to meet at daylight by the chili cannery. Then we split up.

I walked up a street where some ladies were sitting on the front porches in rocking chairs. It was awful nice to sort of stop at each place and size things up and have a little talk. I can't speak much Spanish but did the best I could.

Most of them were pretty nice, considering they didn't hold their favors at any king's ransom. Then I saw this girl in the yellow dress across the street.

I was sure that when I saw her up close she would not be so pretty but I was wrong.

She was one of those people that look good from any angle, far or close.

"Hello, big boy," she said, flashing those teeth and eyes.

"Gosh, honey," I said, "what are you doing down here?"

"Business," she said. "And a good deal of it."

"You ought to be in the movies," I said. "What's your name?"

"Conchita."

"Well, you're certainly mighty pretty," I said.

She wanted to know if my visit was purely social. I said no, that I had been cutting lettuce for a couple of weeks and really needed the love of a good woman.

We discussed more practical matters for a little while.

I went in.

She was really wonderful, this Conchita. Up till about twelve o'clock we spent one of the pleasantest evenings you could imagine. Then those drunks commenced raising hell on the porch.

"Don't notice them," Conchita said. "They'll go away."

But I was irritated.

"I reckon so," I said, "after they've tore down the God damned porch."

I yelled for them to go away but they just sat down on the steps and commenced saying dirty things to us.

I unlocked the door to go run them off but, when I did, they busted on into the house. That really made me mad because I had made the proper arrangements and was the one who belonged to be there.

"I had just as soon try to have a date," I said, "in the Union Depot in St. Louis."

I said I was going to call the cops.

Then the little one hit me with a beer bottle. Naturally it busted and the neck split my nose coming

9

down. I kicked that one hard in the stomach. My leg felt wonderful doing it. He turned white and I'll swear to God his eyes crossed.

He commenced vomiting and when the other one looked to see what was wrong with him I grabbed a certain convenient utensil by the bail and swung on him. This one spread out on the floor just as flat and smooth as varnish.

We tied the two of them up in a bedspread and Conchita lit into them with a broom. I never saw anything funnier in my life. My nose had bled all down my front but I was still glad they had come because it was so nice watching Conchita work on that jumping bedspread with that broom.

We laughed a lot; then Conchita tied my nose up with a string and we rolled the boys out into the yard and went on down to the park.

Next morning we left town on a daylight freight because Jimmy still had not seen any sign. Then Mike, who has always got to say something, said we'd all probably be seeing certain signs in eight or nine days, and this made Jimmy mad.

"God knows," he said, "the Higher Powers have trouble enough keeping from seeing our faults without you mixing them up in your lecherous allusions."

Mike said he was sorry.

We talked about the things that had happened last night.

Mike said he just picked the first one he came to because he figured there would be plenty of better times to walk up and down streets looking on porches.

I guess they thought I never was going to stop when I got started on Conchita.

Finally Mike says, "Not doubting nobody's word, but if what you're saying was ten per cent true, you'd still be back there in San Antonio." Then he turns to Jimmy and says, "How about you, Jimmy?"

For a long time Jimmy just sat there sort of mooning. But even when he moons like this, there is nearly always a warm little twinkle in his eye.

"I guess I didn't do so terrible bad," he said. "I struck up with a Mrs. Gonzales, a widow lady. Maybe she was not as elegant as Conchita but she had a pan full of the best chicken dumplings I ever ran across. And I don't want to seem boastful but...well, I still got my dollar."

So when we pulled into Taylor, which is a division point and where they change engines, Jimmy said, "It ain't often such good fortune comes my way, at least not to the tune of a big silver dollar. You boys worked hard cutting that lettuce and I'd like to show my appreciation. Let's just step across the street and tilt a chili, as you might say, for auld lang syne."

This kind of thing just kills Mike. He ducked his head.

"Jesus, Jimmy," I said, "you don't owe us nothing for snipping up those few little old bunches of lettuce."

It is things like this that make us willing to beg for this guy and even work.

I remember the time that big Greek down in the Imperial Valley tried to take Jimmy's tobacco away from him and Mike whipped him right down to the

11

ground with that bunch of beets. I think we thought he was dead and ran.

But Jimmy didn't say anything more until we walked in and sat down at the counter. Then he says, "Bring these boys two red chilis and two cold beers and the fattest, freshest package of ready rolls in the house. And if there's any of that chili left, I'll take a bowl myself."

We got back on that train feeling like the Rockefeller boys.

"Jimmy could have slipped that dollar by us," Mike said, admiring.

Jimmy was picking his teeth with a matchstick.

"It was nothing but a liability," he said, picking. "A silver dollar in your shoe makes walking bad and friendship incomplete. And if it stays there long enough, it will grow a corn on your foot and a little wart on your heart."

Then he rolled the old green plaid coat into a pillow and took himself a nap.

It must have been about three that afternoon when it happened. Mike was over in the corner asleep. I was laying on my back humming an awfully dirty old song. And Jimmy was making crows'-feet with a piece of string, when the engineer slammed on the air.

Mike woke up and said, "What the hell?"

"Must've hit something," I says.

It was a long train. We were pretty close to the caboose. Our door was open about a foot and when we stopped Mike went over and looked out.

"We're on a bridge," he said. Then, looking down by the track, he said, "Jesus!"

"What's the matter?" I asked.

12

"We hit somebody."

Jimmy and me went to the door and looked out. There the man was laying on the ground. A minnow seine was laying close to him and you could see where he was camping over under the highway bridge. There was a skiff and a cot and a fire going under an iron pot. You never saw a nicer camp anywhere.

I guess the poor guy had been walking across the trestle on his way to seine some bait. He wasn't ten feet from our door, and on one of his hands, which was still in pretty good shape, there was a blue tattooed star, just like the red one on Jimmy's hand.

All the back part of the train was still on the bridge.

"This must be the Brazos, ain't it?" Mike said.

"Yeah," I said. "Where you going, Jimmy?"

"Over here to set on this rock," Jimmy said.

By the time the train crew got there the man that got hit was cold dead. For a long time nobody noticed Jimmy sitting over on the rock crying.

"What the hell's the matter with him?" the conductor asked.

At first Jimmy didn't say anything. Then he looked up and said, "Wouldn't you feel bad to see your own flesh and blood get its life snuffed out by a freight train?"

"You mean he was your kinfolks?" the engineer asked.

"Just my brother," Jimmy says. "See that star on his hand? That's our family mark."

"Well, it's sure too bad," the conductor said.

The engineer took his cap off and put it in his hip pocket and started rolling a cigarette.

"I'll swear I never done it on purpose," he said. "There's just no place I can run this thing except down the track."

"I don't hold any hard feeling toward you boys," Jimmy said.

"Well, what you want us to do with him?" the conductor asked.

"Just leave him here," Jimmy said, "where loving hands can bury him."

"If you want to keep him, we'll get on down the line," the conductor said, "so we can let Number Three through."

Jimmy gave the conductor his name and said his dead brother's name was Eric. The conductor said he'd turn it in.

When the train was gone Mike said, "Well, what are we gonna do with Brother Eric?"

Jimmy was still sitting on the rock where he had been crying. But now he seemed to have pretty good control over himself.

"One of you boys just step over there and set that kettle off the fire," he said. "It's a sin to burn up good food. . . . Maybe you better taste it, Mike, and see how it's seasoned. You know I like lots of black pepper."

When Mike came back he brought a shovel.

"How was the stew?" Jimmy said.

"Pretty good," Mike said. "Beef. I just wish he'd left them God damned turnips out of it. . . . Want me to start digging?"

"I guess not."

"Well, what are we gonna do with Eric?" I said.

"I've thought about it," Jimmy says, "and that

14

ground looks mighty hard. Mike, you get some wire and a big rock and we'll bury Eric at sea."

Mike said we ought not to bury Eric since we might need him for evidence.

But Jimmy said, "No, Mike. It ain't practical in this weather. Besides, the train crew has done witnessed him once and you can run that witnessing into the ground."

So we buried poor Eric in the river like we set out to do and went on over to the camp.

Chapter Two

This camp was really nice. The bridge that it was under was old but the floor had been covered with tarvia, so naturally it wouldn't leak. There were two wooden boxes hanging on a wire with tin plates and cups and knives and forks in them. In one there was two loaves of stale bread and some onions and potatoes and a bucket of grease and some salt and pepper and coffee and molasses. And since it was hung on wire like that, there weren't any ants at all. There was also an extra-good butcher knife made out of an old saw blade, and a single-shot twelve-gauge shotgun and three shells in the grub box.

The bridge ran east and west high up over the river so that the camp was better than fifteen feet above the water. Besides, there was plenty of room for the south breeze to sweep through. But before I forget it, there was also an oil lantern with a dirty chimney and nearly a gallon of kerosene and an old ax with a wired up handle.

17

I guess the river must have been about two hundred feet wide at the camp. There was a long, broad sand bar on our side and rock cliffs on the other side running straight up about twenty feet. Up the river a little way it forked, one fork running north and one east. And down at the first bend below us there was an island. I'd say about a quarter of a mile below us. It was long and sort of curving, about the shape of a raw weenie, a hundred yards long by about thirty yards wide.

"If we ever get in any trouble," I said, "we can hide on that island."

"Naturally," Jimmy says, "the Higher Powers wouldn't send us to a place that didn't provide for emergencies. I guess they know better than anybody that the flesh is weak and the best resolves sometimes crumble."

Mike dished out three plates of stew and some of that stale bread. Then we sat down on the cot and started eating. Jimmy kept standing up.

"What's the matter, Jimmy?" I said. "You got a boil on your hind end?"

"No," Jimmy said. "That old canvas on the cot looks pretty rotten. I don't see how it's holding you two up as it is."

"All right," Mike said, "let's get up. We don't want to bust Jimmy's bed."

Jimmy just grinned and sat down in the sand. "You boys are sure nice to me," he said.

Mike went over and got him some more stew.

While we were eating, Mike said, "Ain't that water I see in the bottom of that old skiff?"

I said it was.

Then Mike began to cuss Eric and said a leaky skiff

18

was an abomination before God and he never liked any-body that owned one and now he knew how come Eric to sit down on the track.

But Jimmy said that was no way to speak about our late lamented benefactor and let's take a look at the neighborhood. Besides, he said, the water in the bottom of that old skiff would be a wonderful place for me and Mike to wash dishes.

Not far up the sand bar we found a spring of pretty good water. It ran about a four-inch stream of clear cool bubbly water down a little channel of clean gravel. Also there was water cress growing in the spring which the running water rippled like a woman's hair in the breeze.

Over on the high bank we saw a woman herding what looked like a hundred turkeys.

At the sight of these turkeys Jimmy grinned big and broad and of course made us feel good. Then he says the first time we go to the store we'd better get a nick-el's worth of garlic. Without garlic, he says, the dressing tastes flat.

When we walked up onto the bridge we saw a truck farm on one side of the road where somebody was rais-ing tomatoes and cabbage and okra and onions and black-eyed peas and sweet potatoes. On the other side of the road there was a corn and cotton field.

"That truck farm's so perfect," Jimmy says, "that I suspect it of being a mirage."

We argued it wasn't but Jimmy was so certain it was that Mike and me had to go over and pick a bucket of mixed vegetables and bring to him before he'd admit it was real.

19

When we got back from picking he pointed down the road. At the first bend there was a filling station with a sign on it that said: "Gasoline. Groceries. Beer. Ice. Catfish."

For a little while we all just stood there looking.

"I wish you hadn't said what you did about Eric," Jimmy says to Mike. "He has left us many good things."

"I guess so," Mike said, "but he could just as well patched that old skiff as not."

It was late afternoon but the sun was still beating down strong and hot.

"I don't claim to be any smarter than the next man," I said, "but there's one thing I've always noticed."

"What's that?" Mike said.

"Well," I said, "it's just this: it looks like a man can get thirstier under a bridge than nearly anywhere on earth."

"I never give it no thought," Mike said, "but it does seem to be true."

"And what's more," I said, "it don't make me especially thirsty for spring water."

"I've been thinking," Jimmy says, "about the time that Mr. Mattocks, the hardware man in our town, shot his best customer by accident showing him a gun. . . . We're all happy now and good friends but there may come a time when we will lose patience with each other. That old shotgun just ought not to be down there."

"You mean swap it for beer?" I said.

"That's one way of getting rid of a menace," Jimmy says. "Would you like to run get the shotgun, Mike?"

"Sure," Mike says.

20

"And bring those three shells," Jimmy said. "They might make the difference of a bottle."

We walked on down the road till we came to the store. When we went in the proprietor was down behind the back counter rolling something that rattled with three Negroes and a Mexican.

When he stuck his head up over the counter he saw the shotgun and raised both hands. The Negroes and the Mexican crawled on out the back door.

The storekeeper was about five and a half feet tall. He had one eye that didn't work and was the kind of man that's always sweating.

Jimmy just grinned at him.

"Friend," he said, "if you think we've come in here to burgle your store, you're all wrong. All we intend to do is be neighbors and customers."

"Oh," the storekeeper said, grinning in a way that made me glad he didn't owe us any money.

"We're living down under the bridge," Jimmy said, "and mean to carry on my brother's fishing business."

"Is ole Sam Rutherford your brother?"

"Poor Sam," Jimmy said. "He was up until about three o'clock this afternoon when he contested that fast freight for the right of way."

"Too bad," old Gotch-Eye said. "I got my fish from him."

"Oh, me and my friends here, Eddie and Mike, will carry on the fish business just the same."

"You catch 'em and I'll sell 'em," Gotch said.

"By the way," Jimmy said, "Sam and I was talking this morning and we went over the account book together."

"Book?"

"Didn't you know Sam put those things down in a book?"

"No, I didn't."

"Well anyway, we'll be willing to take it out in trade."

"Take what out in trade?"

"That little amount you owed Sam for those fish."

"How much was it?"

"I'd have to step down to the bridge," Jimmy says, "and get the book."

"Well, I'll make you a proposition," the storekeeper said. "I'll settle with you boys for what baloney and cheese and crackers you care to eat and what beer you'd like to drink between now and closing time."

"Uncap three cold ones," Jimmy says. "My throat is caked with this Brazos Bottom dust. . . . And by the way, I guess you're still closing at the regular time."

"Sure. Eight o'clock."

"That ain't what Sam said."

"All right then. Ten."

You could write your name in the frost on those brown bottles.

I know it must have made Jimmy's teeth ache because he just tilted that first bottle up to his mouth and let every bit of the beer run out.

We had had three apiece when Mike said, "What about the shotgun, Jimmy?"

"We must grease it and cherish it," Jimmy says. "As long as we keep it, it will protect us from harm. A shotgun is good against burglars and intruders. It will sweeten the nature of the surliest husbands. And finally," he said, "it will always swap for this fluid amber delight."

"By God," Mike says, "it's wonderful how that man can talk and how good that talk can make you feel."

"What our lives would have been without him," I said, "I shudder to think about."

"Here," Jimmy said, modest, trying to turn it off like nothing had happened, "eat some cheese."

The store keeper's name was Newt Tabor and he agreed to pay us ten cents a pound for all the catfish we could catch. But he said we'd have to leave the skin and heads on because his customers had complained about Sam's catfish steaks being gar meat.

About six o'clock a woman came downstairs that Newt said was his wife, Fanny. Fanny said for him to go on upstairs, that his supper was on the table getting cold and she would tend to the store. He told her we were supposed to get all the beer we wanted and went on up.

Fanny was not exactly a Cleopatra but things like that just don't bother Mike. In almost no time he was asking when her husband goes to town because it would be nice to have somebody to ride with. Also, does she ever stroll down to the river and does she like to ride in a skiff?

She was terribly put out when she heard about Sam. First she said it was on account of he caught such nice fish and then because he was such a good customer.

Finally Jimmy says, "I guess your husband was in the store all day, wasn't he?"

But it seems that she doesn't want to answer this question straight and we order three more cold ones.

Anyway, when closing time came we were feeling pretty good. Old Newt had done a lot of worrying after we'd finished the first case at about a quarter after seven.

"Ain't you afraid you boys'll get sick?" he had said.

"I reckon every man has got just so much sickness planned out for him," Jimmy had said, "and if we can work off a little of ours by drinking this good cold beer, that ought to be about as good a way as any."

When ten o'clock came there were thirty-nine empties sitting on the counter and cheese rinds and baloney skins all over everything. Newt was fixing to close up when a car drove up outside for gas.

While Newt was filling it Jimmy got to talking to the driver and found out that Newt had run the clock up on us forty minutes. So when he came back we drank a half dozen more that we really didn't crave because Jimmy said it was our duty to do what we could to mend Newt's crooked ways.

Then we started on up the road.

It was a nice clear night. The south breeze was blowing and the moon was coming up big and orange over on the other side of the truck farm. It was really wonderful walking down that road full of beer to your own camp.

Mike cried a little bit and now he altogether forgave Sam for the leaky skiff and said he guessed any man that had to put up with that crooked son of a bitch of a Newt Tabor wouldn't have time to keep his boat in really first-class shape. Mike said that crookedness on the part of his fellows just broke his heart and that, while that last six bottles of beer we drank on Newt was a step in the right direction, it was not enough. The trouble with Newt, he said, was he had no responsibility. His home was desolate and the yard empty.

"Ain't it," he demanded, "any woman's sacred right to be a mother?"

We said it was. Then Mike said that if we stayed here any time at all he meant to perform certain actions that would better fit him to meet his Maker in case the candle of his own soul should get blown out unexpectedly like Sam's.

I remarked that there was a world of the preacher in Mike, and Jimmy said that he seemed to have absolutely all the qualifications except maybe religion.

Then we commenced talking about poor Sam's fate and what a perishable thing this life really was.

Maybe, Mike said, he had committed some great sin.

"And if I'm any judge," Jimmy says, "he committed it in the back of the store while old Newt had gone for the ice."

"That ain't no sin," Mike said.

"The Bible says it is," I said.

"Well, anybody makes mistakes — even the Bible," Mike said. "It's a wonderful thing and I'm for it. . . . Besides, from what I hear, there was a world of it went on back in Bible times."

"But it was frowned on," I said.

"Only by them," Mike said, "that had gone after the ice."

"Anyway," Jimmy says, "it goes to prove what I always said. I mean about Brother Sam getting hit by the train."

"What have you said?" we said.

"That everything turns out for the best if you get there in time."

"I don't see no best in it for Sam," Mike says.

"Somebody's got to get the worst of everything," Jimmy said. "For instance now, when we catch a three-pound fish. That's bad for the fish. But at Newt's store it turns into three cold bottles of beer and that's good. One fish suffers to gladden three hearts. So we come out two hearts ahead. You understand that, don't you?"

"I do," Mike said, "so long as I ain't the fish nor poor Sam."

"Well, look at another angle of it," Jimmy said. "We all know that Newt Tabor is an evil man. He tried to rob us of our inheritance and then turned the clock up to cheat us out of a measly six bottles of beer that he gets at cost. Now when he left the store this morning he got him a club and sat down behind a bush on the trail leading to Sam's bait grounds. When Sam came by he conked him and set him on the track. Right there a shallow person would have said evil has come out ahead. Poor Sam, who has never done a thing wrong more than give Fanny what consolation he could, has perished and wickedness is the top dog in these Bottoms.

"Then we came on the scene and discovered our brother. We collected Sam's just debt from old Newt. And for Fanny certain pleasures that perished on the tracks with Sam will be multiplied a hundredfold by the thoughtful little attentions of our friend Mike."

"By God," Mike said, "it's a wonderful thing how you figure things out!"

"No, it's not," Jimmy said, "it's as plain as day. Walls

26

rise up out of the earth to protect the pure in heart. At times, when it was necessary, light bread has been known to fall out of the sky. Virtue is like a worm that grows three new heads every time you chop one off."

Then Mike turned to me and said, "By Jesus, I had never realized what good men we were."

"Me either," I said, "but don't it make you feel wonderful?"

We had almost reached the bridge when Jimmy said, "What's that black hunk of something over there?"

"Looks like a monument," I said.

We struck some matches and looked.

It was a big piece of granite with a copper plate on it that said:

Brazos River Forks Called by the Ancient Spaniards
Los Dos Brazos de Dios

"They called it 'The Two Arms of God'!" Jimmy says. "That's where we drifted to and where we lit."

I said it looked like a miracle and Mike cried some more.

Then Jimmy says, "Is that sign enough for you boys?"

Mike was still bellowing but I said it was.

As we went on down to the camp Jimmy said, "It would be a shame to sleep on such a fine night as this and after our wonderful experience with the Higher Powers' sign and old Newt's beer. If anybody cares to bail the boat out, I'll hold the lantern while you boys run the lines, because there may be fish on them this minute."

We were anxious to go, too, so we lit the lantern and bailed out the skiff and started off.

27

When we had about reached the place where we'd dumped Sam in, Jimmy took a little third-grown sunflower blossom out of his pocket. He had picked it on the way from the store. The lantern light was on his face and I saw he was smiling awfully big and warm and tender as he said, "Dear Sam, this one little ditch flower, common though it be, in our hearts represents ten thousand roses. You have laid down your life in our welfare. You have strewn our path with camps and cots and accounts owed and one of the best God damned stews it has ever been my privilege to eat. So now, little train-hit friend, rest peacefully. Our gratitude will keep you warm. For the last time we salute you with this blanket of roses."

He dropped the flower into the water.

I didn't say anything and neither did Mike but I heard him sniffle.

Then with his voice clear and fine, Jimmy says, "All right, boys, row on up the river."

Chapter Three

It was breaking day when we got in from running the lines. We had found about seventy-five of them and I guess old Sam had baited them that morning because we took off something better than twenty pounds of fish and brought them back to the live box, which is sort of a big underwater cage that you put fish in so they'll stay alive. There was nearly fifteen pounds already in it.

After we let Jimmy out on the sand bar we pulled the skiff out and Mike said, "Let's go on up and hit the hay."

Me and Mike was tired. We had rowed about five miles all told. Our hands were blistered and our backs sore.

"You boys go ahead and get some rest," Jimmy said. "I got to stay up and see the sun rise."

It was nice, all right, there on that sand bar with the

sky turning gray up above the east bank. You know how still it can get a lot of times right at dawn. The river was just like a piece of slick gray glass, and there seemed to be something a little strange and ghostly about Jimmy walking along the sand bar carrying that old lighted lantern. I couldn't tell you why it is but there's something funny about watching a lantern burn while dawn is breaking. In fact I always feel like it really ain't dawn yet till that lantern is blown out. In the first place, you get used to it being the center of everything at night down on the river and it seems kind of strange to watch stuff coming into sight out of range of the lantern light.

A couple of big gars rolled over the top of the water just like they wanted to get a good look around. Then a lot of turtles began sticking their heads up and I know good and well that's what they wanted.

Suddenly Jimmy turned around and said, "I'll tell you what. Let's go swimming."

"In the name of God," Mike said, "what for?"

"Well," Jimmy says, "it's like this. This is our new home. And what I mean, I really like it. I like it so much that I reckon I just kind of want to wallow in it. You don't feel like a really good lodge member, do you, till you've rode the goat? Nor you ain't no part of a Baptist till you've gone down over your head in holy water? . . . I just figured we'd feel more like we belonged here if we took a little swim."

Naturally we saw the point to this at once and realized nobody on earth but Jimmy would have seen the sentiment in the thing like that and put it into words so good.

Mike shucked off his clothes.

"I'm God damned near dead," he said, "but if Jimmy wants us baptized I reckon we might as well hit it."

So in we went and stuck around till Jimmy got to see the sun come up.

Then we turned in.

We woke up about five that afternoon and made some coffee. But when Jimmy went to get a drink and there wasn't any water, I took the bucket and went off down to the spring.

It was about a hundred yards down the bank and of course a lot of willows had grown up around it. Somebody had dug a hole about a yard deep and put a piece of tile well curbing just in front of the spring so that it was handy to dip a bucket in.

I guess I must not have been good awake because I came in an ace of stepping on a woman's hand. She was sitting there with her dress pulled up over her thighs and her feet down in that joint of well curbing.

First it sort of scared me. But when I got a good look at her I decided then and there she would do for me. She was somewhere along in her twenties and pretty as a picture. She put me in mind of a real ripe plum that you pick quick because you know if you don't the birds will get it. And not only that. She also had something that got you to sort of panting just from looking at her.

"Oh," she said, pulling her feet out of the spring and sitting down on them. "My feet was hot."

We were both kind of flustered. I really didn't have time to think of anything very good to say so I just says, "Lady, don't apologize to me. That water will always taste better to me for having been flavored by those two dainty feet."

She laughed and said, "You're mighty nice. What are you doing down here?"

"Oh, me? I'm living up under the bridge. I have taken over Sam's fishing business. . . . You married?"

"Yeah," she said. "I'm Frank's wife. He's the one that's working that cotton and corn. . . . Anybody with you?"

"Yes," I said, "a couple of friends. I've got 'em down here trying to cure them."

"Of what?"

"Well," I said, "it really ain't the sort of thing I'd like to say out loud before a lady."

"Pore things," she said. "I can certainly sympathize with 'em."

"Now looky here," I said. "You don't mean you've already. . . ."

She laughed. That laugh put you in mind of a puppy running up stairsteps.

"Goodness, no," she said, and knocked on a piece of driftwood with her knuckles. "I was just remembering how pore Uncle Gus used to holler and carry on." She laughed again. "I guess it really ain't a laughing matter," she said, "but I was remembering that day the pore thing run off of the back porch with that hand ax, heading for the shed, and us girls all hollered but he just kept running and no telling what'd happened if Frank hadn't throwed a chunk that caught him in the back of the head."

"It's a terrible thing," I said. "But it makes you glad

32

of having led a good clean life. . . . Do you come down here about this time every day?"

She said she did.

"I don't guess Frank would mind us just watering here together, would he?"

"Frank's sweet," she said, "but he stays awful busy with his crop."

"Do you believe in love at first sight?" I says.

"I never thought about it much."

"Well," I says, "do you like catfish?"

"Yes sir-ree," she said.

"I'll have you some here tomorrow night."

A big dreamy smile came on her face.

"I think you're beautiful," I said.

"You better bring at least four pounds," she said. "Frank can eat nearly three."

"You reckon Frank would shoot me if I kissed you?"

"The truth to tell," she said, "Frank's an awful poor shot."

Now she was standing up and was many times more handsome in some respects.

Real gently, like you go about bridling a wild horse, I reached for her.

She jumped back.

"What's the matter?" I said.

She just looked at me, smiling, kind of out of breath. This time when she jumped I took out after her, running, but I tripped on a willow root and fell down.

For a minute she stood in the edge of the willows laughing. Then she threw me a kiss.

"Don't forget my catfish tomorrow," she said and walked out into the open.

I wanted to choke her, to bust her in the jaw, almost as much as anything.

What makes women do things like that?

I dipped up my water and left.

When I got back to the bridge Mike had already skinned three catfish and was dropping them in a skillet of hot grease.

"We had about give you up," Jimmy says from the cot.

"Can't a man have a little privacy to tend to his personal needs?" I said.

And Mike says, "Well, Eddie, it looks like to me you could find somewhere besides right at the spring."

But before long we were eating channel cat fried good and brown and when we finished Mike says, "Hadn't we better go rustle up some bait?"

"What's the hurry?" I said.

"That damned ole Newt closes at ten o'clock," Mike said, "and we got to catch bait and bait out the lines. If we fool around here long enough we'll just about have to make the night plum sober."

So I took one end of the minnow seine, a thirty-footer, which is ten feet longer than legal, and Mike took the other end. Jimmy said he'd carry the bucket.

Now maybe you never have seined any bait. If you're tired to begin with, and maybe sleepy, it's awful. But when you've just waked up and it's late in the afternoon, and you've got a belly full of catfish and stale bread, and when you've got a nice level half-mile-long sand bar with no rocks in it to hurt your feet, then it's really wonderful. Maybe you get naked, or at the most, leave your britches on. The water is cool and clean feeling and then when you get the seine stretched you bow your back and give it hell, digging your toes in the sand so the weight of the other man's pull don't jerk you off your feet. A thirty-foot seine pulls awful heavy but it catches bait, and if you want to, instead of pushing the stick, you can swing your back end around and pull it and really get some power out of your legs.

I don't guess we got over ten good ones that first haul. By good ones I mean as big as a man's finger and bigger. But that's enough to bait ten hooks. And after all, there is nothing, I reckon, that makes you feel better than the sight of good minnows flipping a seine. Of course good bait is not a guarantee of a good catch but at least you know you are getting somewhere when you see a lot of plump little silver flips as the seine comes out of the water.

Naturally on such a big sand bar the minnows are scattered. But like I say, we were fresh from sleeping and the water felt good, so we kept on making one drag after another. Then we'd gather up the minnows in our hands and carry them to Jimmy's bucket.

I guess we made thirty drags but we certainly had a pretty bucketful of minnows.

Then we floated the skiff, and me and Mike rolled a cigarette and Jimmy lit his pipe, and off we went up the river.

Most folks think it takes a lot of rowing to get up a river but it really doesn't. Especially on a wide one with a good current like the Brazos. Because nearly everywhere there is a main channel on one side or the other and on the side where the channel isn't there's an eddy flowing, maybe not as fast, but steady, upstream. So when you want to go up, you just switch from one eddy to the other and if you're not in a hurry you don't have to do any rowing at all.

We just sat there smoking, me guiding and Mike in front baiting, taking off a fish every once in a while that got caught on a piece of leftover bait. Jimmy said he'd keep the water bailed out of the boat. But it was awfully hard for him to keep his mind on things as uninteresting as that.

"You know," Jimmy says, sitting there watching the shadows spread out over the river, "this baiting-up is like planting seeds in the soil. You just do it and wait, and then you come back about daylight and that bait has increased into a good eating fish.

"Except," Mike says, "where them damn turtles and gars steals it."

"Naturally," Jimmy says, "there are always good crops and bad. But the part I like is, you don't have to wait all summer, like on cotton, and there ain't no weeds to hoe in the hot sun. You just wait one night. It all happens in the dark down in the bowels of the river. I reckon it's the mystery of it mostly that's appealing."

"What I like," Mike says, "is to see the poles pulling so you know you've got one on that line and how big is he."

By now we had started back down the channel. When we came to the big trotline Mike says, "How about you holding on to the line, Jimmy, while I bait the hooks?"

Jimmy said all right. He was doing very well at it till a sort of whirlpool caught the boat and spun it around sideways. Then the current hit us broadside and yanked

36

the line through Jimmy's hand until the first hooks came by and caught in his thumb and dragged him out of the boat.

It nearly scared me and Mike to death. That current was terribly strong and there was Jimmy flouncing around among all those hooks. We had taken drowned fish off those very hooks because the current caught in their mouths and choked them.

The damned boat was still sideways, bouncing along on the fast water, and it seemed like I never would get it straight.

That old trotline was weighted with about fifteen pounds of iron.

Jimmy went out of sight.

Now Mike was rowing with all his might and the thought flashed through my mind of the catfish eating Jimmy like they already had poor Sam. It made me sick but we kept on fighting that current till Mike's oar hit something hard which happily was Jimmy's head. Mike snatched at it and caught Jimmy's collar and swung on. Then the current against the boat made that hook cut through the end of Jimmy's thumb and another hook he'd picked up ripped out of his britches leg and Mike pulled him in the boat.

Jimmy was fish-belly white, and of course out, but Mike worked with him while I drove for the sand bar.

After about ten minutes hard work on him he opened his eyes.

Then he grinned weak and said, "I'd sort of expected to see old Sam instead of you boys."

Back at the camp we tied up Jimmy's thumb with a rag and poured kerosene on it. I got all the fish out of the live box except three, which I tied on a string and hid for Frank's wife, and we started for the store.

Newt tried to get us to take five dollars for the fish but Jimmy made him give us six. Then he wormed it out of Newt that he sold whisky without a license and we gave him two and a half for a quart. But we didn't open it there. We drank a dozen beers to take the edge off our thirst and bought a piece of bacon and some tobacco. Then we borrowed a sack, to gather some vegetables in on the way home, and left.

Down at the bridge after we'd drunk about a pint, Jimmy says, "Boys, I been communing with my conscience."

"Is that so?" Mike says, "What about?"

"Catching those poor fish on hooks."

"Look Jimmy," I said. "We're sorry about your thumb but if we don't catch no fish we don't eat, let alone drink."

"I have told both of you," Jimmy says, "that virtue properly handled, can nearly always be made to serve some good and useful purpose. Besides, having to seine all that bait every day is a terrible responsibility, and I'm a long ways from wanting another one of them trotline duckin's like I got tonight."

"What can we do?" Mike asked.

"Use fish traps," Jimmy said, "and bait 'em with our neighbor's corn, which needs only picking. Catfish will trail the scent of rank corn for miles. . . . You know what the Bible says."

"In which place?" Mike says.

"That bread cast upon the waters will increase tenfold. Or maybe it's a hundred. Corn is practically the same as bread," Jimmy says, "and would be if you'd grind it up and cook it."

"I know it would swell up," Mike says, "but you wouldn't really have no more bread."

"The hell you wouldn't," Jimmy says. "The Bible says you would. And it don't mean just the same bread swole up."

"We could catch a world of fish all right," I said, "but fish traps are against the law."

"Any law," Jimmy said, "which stands in the way of a humanitarian action don't deserve the notice of honest men. My conscience is law enough for me."

"Me too," Mike said. "It lets you do more."

So we decided to put in fish traps as soon as we could and in the meantime we would not ask Jimmy to hold any more trotlines.

We passed the bottle around.

"How would you boys like to ride down to the island," Jimmy says, "and explore a little?"

By now the moon was up and the south wind was whipping up little waves on the river. The quart had almost gone where that dozen beers had gone and the thought of exploring Weenie Island sounded right adventurous.

"Maybe it's because I'm half-witted," Mike says, "but I don't know what I wouldn't give for a good iron sword to stick in my belt."

Me and Jimmy laughed but finally admitted it would be nice to have one. Then we killed the quart and dumped the water out of the skiff and started down the river.

On the way we talked about buried treasure and

Indian bones but when we got there all we found was some dewberries that were still green and a magneto off of a T-model Ford.

But that was all right with us because Jimmy said Christopher Columbus had about the same luck when he discovered the U.S., except he even wound up in the can.

It was late and we got sleepy. Jimmy had said islands were free territory and whoever spent the night on one established moral title to it even though it had to be held by force of arms in case of a dispute. So we just bedded down in the sand and went to sleep on Weenie Island, which ever afterward we claimed as ours.

Chapter Four

D uring the rest of that first week everything went along about regular. We had reasonable good luck fishing and there was a nice crop of tomatoes getting ripe over at the truck farm.

As for Frank's wife, she and I still had not, as they say in books, been anything to each other. In the first place, that grove of willows at the spring was not more than about fifteen feet thick and she was awfully fleet of foot. I believe she was one of the fastest starters I ever saw. Anyway she and old Frank had eaten fourteen pounds of catfish between them and I figured that ought to be accomplishing something. So I was right patient or, as Jimmy would say, discreet, and never ran beyond the edge of the willow thicket.

Then it rained a good hard rain one day and most of the night. About an hour or two before daylight on this rainy night Mike woke me up and said, "Listen to that."

I listened a minute and said, "He must have slipped off the pavement onto one of those old gummy shoulders."

"I guess so," Mike said.

Then Jimmy woke up and wanted to know what was all the ruckus about.

We told him.

"Maybe we ought to go up and give him a push," I said.

"In this rain?" Mike said.

"Well, I meant have an understanding with him before we started pushing," I said. "How about it, Jimmy?"

"That rain sounds mighty wet," Jimmy said. "I guess the thing to do is let them decide it."

"The car folks?" Mike says.

"Hell no," Jimmy says, "the Higher Powers."

"You mean," Mike says, "that they'll send us another one of them old tombstones with writing on it?"

"Certainly not," Jimmy says. "They'll just have it stop raining. That ought to be sign enough for anybody."

We rolled some Durham and smoked, waiting on the sign. About twenty minutes later we got it.

We walked barefooted up to the bridge approach where the car had slipped off. The man was still spinning the wheels.

"Seems like you're doing a lot of traveling," Jimmy said, "and not getting nowhere."

Suddenly, plain scared, the man reached his hand in the car pocket and left it there.

"We just meant to see if you wanted a push," Jimmy said.

"Get away from this car," the man said, quick, flustered. Then he said, "Wait a minute."

He didn't know what he wanted.

Jimmy turned and gave us the eye.

It was nice for somebody else to be on the spot for a change instead of us.

"What's the matter, bud?" Mike said. "Ku Klux after you?"

"No," he said. "I just got excited — being stuck and all."

I put my head in the other window.

"What's that you got in the back under that wagon sheet?" I said.

"Nothing," he said. Then he said, "Just some dogs."

"Well," I said, "that's the first time I ever heard dogs mumbling Dutch. Or maybe it's Latin."

He pulled his gun.

"God damn it," he said, "back away."

"Friend," Jimmy said, "you're talking mighty biggetty for somebody that's stuck in the mud and has got a whole back seat full of escaped convicts."

The man threw the gun back in the car pocket.

"I don't never have no luck," he said.

It was kind of pitiful but we sure had him where we wanted him.

He pulled the stopper out of a pint of whisky and said, "Drink?"

It got to Mike last and he swore there was just a sip in it.

"Now, friend," Jimmy says, "we've caught you with your britches at your knees. You might just as well pour your heart out to us."

"All right," the man said. "I'll even make you a proposition. I brought that fellow in from Mexico. Maybe he doesn't have any passport or has not been passed by the immigration authorities. But he's a nice fellow and if you'll take him off my hands, just keep him out of circulation for a week until I can get away, I'll give you a ten-dollar bill."

We waited for Jimmy to say.

"Mr. Smuggler," Jimmy said, "you can't know how hard we try to live within the law. Many times we have been weak or necessity has forced us into certain little discrepancies. But now we have a nice camp. There's catfish in the live box and vegetables across the road, so that ten dollars, I'm thankful to say, cannot deprive us of our honor or our respect for the law. Besides, it ought to be worth more than that to you to get rid of him."

"Twelve and a half."

"I'd as soon sin for ten."

"Fourteen."

"Time is money," Jimmy said. "Name your best price."

"A twenty-dollar bill. And you boys push me out of the mud."

"Open that back door," Jimmy says, "and turn him out. He can help us push."

That's how we got Oof.

We pushed the man out of the mud and led Oof, which just seemed the natural thing to call him, down to the camp. He was about six and a half feet tall and kind of black and kind of red and weighed enough to bust the scales.

"What's your name?" Jimmy asked him.

He made a racket but that racket didn't make sense.

"My God," Mike said, "he can't even talk."

"Mike," Jimmy said, "he is our guest, dues paid in full; you must be patient. He talks all right. He just ain't broke to English."

But we dogged him until we found out that he knew a few words of English.

"Where you from?" Mike said.

"Home," Oof said.

"I knew that," Mike said, "Where's home?"

But he couldn't handle this. He just kept on saying home, his eyeballs as big as doorknobs. It was funny to us that while Oof talked pretty fair pigeon English he was this weak on geography.

But he caught on fast to who we were. By good daylight you could point at Jimmy and say, "Who's that?" and he'd say, "Jimmy," or me and he'd say, "Eddie," or him and he'd say, "Oof." But when we'd point at Mike he'd just die laughing.

"What's the matter with that heathen son of a bitch?" Mike said. "Is he crazy?"

"No," I says, "he's just got a good sense of humor."

This made Mike mad and he says to me, "Do you want to have both eyes slapped into one?"

I knew he could do it.

"No thanks," I said.

"Then lay off me. This Hottentot don't know no better but you do."

"O.K.," I said. "I guess that extra foot of height he's got don't have anything to do with it."

Mike picked up a boat oar but before he could swing it Jimmy says, "Eddie's only playing. And don't start no excitement or that orangoutang'll pull us to pieces."

But Oof stayed pretty peaceable. Naturally we were careful to keep from getting him excited.

Then he started pointing to his stomach and rubbing it.

"Oof hungry," he said.

"What do you reckon they eat where he comes from?" Mike said.

We didn't know so Jimmy said cook him some fish.

I built a fire and Mike got three one-pounders out of the live box. We decided to boil them because it was less trouble and would save grease, which Jimmy said might upset Oof's savage insides.

"Let's just drop 'em in like they are," Mike says. "He probably don't know they ought to be cleaned."

But Jimmy said no and we had to dress them. When those were gone Oof set up a howl till we boiled three more and gave him another loaf of bread.

After he devoured these he grinned at each one of us separately, then just relaxed and lay down and went to sleep.

That appetite he had worried us but what could we do?

Anyway we debated the question, Resolved that: Mike Ought to Go to the Store for Whisky, and it turned out two to one in favor of the Positive.

A little while after we woke up Jimmy said, "Boys,

we have been trusted with Oof's education. We have abetted his fly-by-night entrance into this land. It is our duty to make a good citizen of him."

"What can you make out of a hyena?" Mike said.

"The greatest lesson," Jimmy said, "is industry. Idleness welcomes the devil's influence. We must make him proficient in such useful tasks as rowing boats, gathering wood and bait — "

"I thought we was gonna build fish traps," I said.

". . . also in carpentry," Jimmy says, "and abstinence."

"Christ yes," Mike says. "He would drink us out of house and home."

"In recompense," Jimmy says, "he will gain eloquence in the language, learn the trade of fishing —"

"And dish- and clothes- and backwashing," Mike said.

"Yes," Jimmy says, "we must guard him from all the pitfalls into which we have fallen, make him a first class citizen in every respect."

"Looks like to me," Mike said, "he's hard enough to stand as it is."

"There's wisdom and foresight in what you say, Mike," Jimmy says. "If we do our duty and teach him all the virtues of drudgery and chinchiness and all the stuffy conceits of respectability, he'll make mighty tiresome company."

"That's all right," I said, trying to be a ray of sunshine. "We're the boys that can take it."

While we had been talking we had drunk the last quart bought with the Oof money and Mike must have been feeling wonderful.

47

"Let's jump on him," he says.

But Jimmy said fisticuffs had no part in the training of a useful citizen. Who did we think we were, Hitler or Mussolini? He recited a poem about the white man's burden. I held up but of course Mike cried. Oof just grinned and patted Jimmy's bald spot.

Then Sunday came and there wasn't anything else to do, so Mike says, "Let's make a Christian out of Oof."

That sounded all right to me.

"Go to it," I said.

Jimmy was asleep or, of course, we'd have turned the job over to him.

"You heard about God?" Mike says.

"Sure," Oof said. "Want see Him?"

This scared Mike. He didn't know what to say.

Oof pulled a round rock with a hole in the middle of it out of his pocket. The rock was about as big as a good-sized apple. There was a rawhide thong a foot long tied through the hole.

"Him God," Oof says.

"Aw hell," Mike says. Then he says, "Listen, Oof. God is the big boss man. He's got whiskers and, what I mean, plenty of authority. He lives up in the sky."

"That crazy talk," Oof said. "I got God in my pocket."

"You have not," Mike said. "He's up in the sky."

"He no good," Oof said. "Good God don't hide."

"He ain't hiding," Mike yelled. "He lives up there."

Oof wanted to see His house.

"It's too far to see," Mike said.

"Good God live closer to job," Oof said. "What yours good for?"

48

"When you are in a tight place," Mike says, "you pray and He's supposed to get you out. If you get hungry, you pray for grub."

"Tell Him Oof wants bananas."

"I'm not gonna do any such a thing," Mike says. "He can't afford to fool with no three or four bananas."

Oof shook his head.

"I keep mine," he said. "I boss Him. He no boss me. But He strong."

"What can He do?" Mike says.

"Get Oof things. He get me your smokum."

"Tell Him to," Mike says.

Oof grinned. Then he held the rock by the thong and said, "Get Mike's smokum. Amen."

He twirled it on his finger and the rock cracked Mike on the forehead.

When Mike came to, Oof was smoking his cigarette and grinning.

"Now Mike see Oof God strong," he said. "Oof God kiss Mike strong on head."

Then I laughed and Mike ran me off in the river.

Chapter Five

We spent the next few days teaching Oof how to paddle a boat and pull a seine and how to gather vegetables over at the truck farm. Except he had a hard time understanding why the dark of night was any better than when it was moonlight. But Jimmy says all things should be done when the signs are right and that the bright of the moon is a bad sign for vegetable picking just like it is for catching catfish.

Privately Jimmy told us he didn't want to go into the philosophy of the thing with Oof — that is, why we had a right to pick old man Henderson's peas and dig his sweet potatoes — because he figured Oof's simple mind couldn't handle it. But to us he pointed out the likeness between old Henderson and the young rich man in the Bible.

"This young rich man," he says, "had worlds of money but wasn't happy and nothing really set well with him till

51

he gave it all away. Then he had a wonderful time. But old Henderson hasn't got that much sense so we've got to help unburden him of some of his substance."

We understood that so we didn't bother any more about it and gave Oof his woodchopping lesson.

He was pretty bright and caught on all right except we didn't dare turn our backs for fear he'd boil every fish in the live box. Which made it necessary for us to tell him how fine vegetables were for him. They would make him strong and good-looking and the ladies would run after him.

This worked pretty well. There for about a week he just lived on whatever vegetables grew closest to the fence and like to wore out Jimmy's shaving mirror watching to see when he would get handsome.

Then as soon as Oof's lessons let up and we had some free time for conversation and to think things up, Jimmy says, "If I'm any judge of dewberries, those over on Weenie Island ought to be big and plump and ripe by now."

I said I guessed they would but what good were berries without cream or at least milk?

"Well, it's a good hour before old Henderson's milking time," Mike says, "and there's a world of brush in that stock pasture."

"For that matter," Jimmy says, "I reckon that poor cow would be glad to get a-loose from her load a little ahead of time."

We all agreed it would give her lots of relief.

Since the pasture was down the river they said they would drop me off at Weenie Island. Oof was supposed to hold her while Mike did the milking. Jimmy said he'd look out for things at camp. So I got a big bucket and as soon as Oof dumped the water out of the skiff we started down the river.

I got off at the island and went to picking. I had eaten nearly all I could hold and in about thirty minutes I had the bucket half full. Not that that was enough because I knew Oof could eat twice that many unless we could convince him they'd make him sick. But I had slacked up picking and rolled a cigarette and lit it when I heard something moving around not far away.

I just stood there listening. It makes you feel sort of funny when you think you are the only one on an island to hear something moving around. I eased through some bushes to see what it was.

Well, who should it be but Frank's wife, barefooted and cool and pretty looking, stooping over picking berries.

She heard me and looked up. Then she smiled and said, "Hello."

"Honey," I says, "can you swim?"

"Not a lick," she says.

I felt so good I grinned all over.

"Who are you here with?"

"Nobody," she says. "Frank brought me over in the skiff to pick preserving berries."

"And when is he due back?"

"After he unhitches and feeds. 'Bout night, I guess."

I looked up at the sun. It was still a good hour high and there would be another hour of daylight after that. I took off a minute to feel kindly toward Jimmy for wanting berries.

"I guess the catfish have been all right," I said.

"Just as fine as could be," she said. "I told Frank I caught 'em and he says, 'Honey, I don't know what you use for bait but it must be mighty good.'"

"Well," I said, "the last thing on earth I want you to think is that there was any strings whatever attached to those catfish. But that ain't helping me to sleep at night and my appetite has just rolled over and died."

"Maybe you're bilious," she said. "I had a cousin once we thought was blind and the doctor give her some calomel and she got plum all right."

That sort of irritated me, her saying I was bilious, with me leading up to romance. Besides, I was tired of her always dragging in her kinfolks.

"I ain't bilious," I said. "I'm in love."

"Is that so?" she said. Then she said, "And with who, pray tell?"

"You don't know?"

"Uh-uh."

"Well," I said, "she is beautiful like a bunch of flowers. She is built like a bricksmokehouse. To take her in my arms and kiss her, I'd give all my worldly possessions and catch catfish till my eyeballs fell out."

"She is a mighty lucky girl," Frank's wife said.

"But the hell of it," I said, "is she is married to a farmer. And I hesitate to ask her to accept those tender little favors I have in mind."

"What did you have in mind?"

"Well," I said, "just romance, sort of. I have received some mighty high compliments in that line from different ladies. But it is only this queen of my heart that I have the slightest interest in. In a way," I said, "I really

54

have her hemmed up, practically like on an island. But do I look like the kind of man who would use brute force, so long as any other way would work?"

"Call her name."

"You," I said. "You are my heart, my soul, my every desire. You are my sun in the daytime, my moon at night, and always you are a blowtorch running wide open in my insides."

She smiled.

"That's pretty," she said, "just as pretty as can be, and I never heard the old liniment man make a nicer speech. 'Specially what you said about not using force. No woman likes a roughneck. So if you'll turn your back for a minute, I'll give you a surprise."

"What kind of surprise?"

"A nice one," she said. "If you'll just show me the courtesy to turn your back."

"Will you swear you can't swim?" I said.

She swore she couldn't.

So I turned around and shut my eyes.

It was all I could do to get my breath.

After a minute I said, "Ready?"

"Yes," she said and when she did I jumped because it was too far away. When I looked she was out in the river and dewberries were scattered all over the ground.

She waved and threw me a kiss, standing half out of the water; then I knew what she had done. She had emptied my bucket and hers and turned them upside down so they would stay full of air, and pulled them down into the water. Then she had put a foot in the bail of each one and paddled out in the river.

I was so mad I'd of fought a wild cat, or Mike, or

Oof even. The more I looked at those God damned dewberries the madder I got.

I was so mad I wouldn't even wait for the skiff and swam the river and walked on back to camp.

I told Jimmy some Mexicans had hijacked me for my berries.

"Well," Jimmy says, "one of the lightest-colored she-Mexicans I nearly ever saw stopped here a minute ago and left our bucket and told me some medicine to use if I couldn't get relief any other way. She said Mike ought to try it too."

If you would have known anything to say to that, you would have been smarter than me.

"I got to step down to the ditch," I said.

Jimmy just smoked his pipe and kept on making crows' feet with his piece of string.

It was nearly night when Mike and Oof got back. They had had a hard time catching the cow and when they finally hemmed her in the fence corner Oof held her while Mike milked. They had almost a bucketful when old Henderson walked up on them carrying a clean, new, white-ash hoe handle fresh from the store.

Oof jumped the barbed-wire fence but the cow run over Mike, and by the time he got up and tried to cross the fence old Henderson cut down on him with the hoe handle. Every time Mike raised his foot to step on the bottom wire old Henderson would whack him across the seat and Mike would have to put his foot back down. Then he'd whip Mike over the head.

Oof got some clods and tried to chunk old Henderson off but Mike said Oof had more power and the worst aim he ever saw. Mike said he believed Oof would have killed him if he hadn't yelled for him to quit throwing.

Finally, Mike said, he saw old Henderson would never let him over the fence so he just backed up and shut his eyes and dived through it.

Oof said it was the funniest thing he ever saw.

There was some pine tar Sam had left from patching the boat, and Jimmy said if we would mix this with some kerosene and smear it on Mike's cuts (I guess he had two hundred) it would keep the flies from blowing him. So we smeared him good and then all ate some baked sweet potatoes and bacon and Jimmy said that anybody who had sweet potatoes didn't really need any dessert anyway.

Chapter Six

We had never built those fish traps and, I guess, never would if Frank hadn't started coming down to our camp to sit with us at night.

Frank was tall and spare and sort of half-witted and had one of the nicest dispositions you could ask for. We all liked him fine. He was cranky about just three things: snuff and fishhooks and flour. He said Five Dot Garrett snuff was all right for those that liked it, and the same went for Rooster, but so far as he was personally concerned he'd as soon dip coffee grounds as anything besides Tube Rose. In fishhooks it was "sheep shanks." I guess he meant sheepshead hooks. Anyway he wouldn't wet a Pflueger or a Kirby or any other kind. But that flour business nearly killed us. Just as earnest and sober and serious as anything you ever saw, he said any flour besides Gray Dove flour gave him a headache. And whenever he came over to visit with us he always brought a pocketful of biscuits made of Gray Dove, in case we fried any fish.

But as I say, Frank was mighty nice and when he heard we wanted fish traps he said he had an old banana crate at the house and two wire chicken coops that would be the very thing.

Next time he came he brought them with him in the wagon. We all hammered a little and whittled some and got chicken mites on us and by about midnight had three fish traps. We sent Oof after a load of corn and when he got back we baited up.

We put out the traps, which are just any kind of baited boxes or baskets with a funnel-shaped entrance that the fish can't get back out of, and took what fish we had up to Newt's and traded them for whisky and all got drunk.

I just say this to show you that Frank was all right. For instance he was down at the camp the night the old medicine man stopped there. His name was Amos and he had a wagon and a team that he grazed at night, and one of the roundest bellies you ever saw. He wanted to sell us some medicine but we didn't have any money and hated to send him off disappointed, so we asked him to eat supper with us.

In the meantime we sent Oof to the store with the fish and told him to tell Newt to send us two quarts of whisky but explained to Oof that, while it wouldn't hurt us, it made dark-skinned people sick.

After supper we drank some more and Amos told us about standing in a drugstore for twenty years waiting for people to come buy medicine. He was a bachelor and not much of a manager so he had stayed pretty lonesome most of the time. Then one day somebody passed in a trailer and he got thinking how nice it would be just to go where you pleased and meet people and sleep by the road at night. Finally, he said, it got where he had to sleep on the road that night. He just hitched up the team, he said, and loaded the best medicine into the wagon and left the rest for rent and hit the road. It took him about a month to get through expanding and to realize he'd shucked those old pill-smelling store walls off his shoulders. He said he never had been half as happy or met such good people before. I tell you there was some feeling to old Amos. We all knew he would make a good friend.

Then we commenced on the second quart and while we drank it he told us some wonderful experiences he'd had, and when Frank came out with that jolt about all flour but Gray Dove gave him the headache, Amos just caught his breath like a man and did what he could to back Frank up by the rules of medicine.

It was a wonderful conversation and nobody could name anything they'd ever done that either Amos or Jimmy couldn't prove was perfectly right and moral and what their mother would have wanted them to do.

By now the whisky was gone but since it had to go sometime, this did as well as any because we were all good and drunk. Then Amos stood up and said, "Boys, we have met here by this river for a few sweet hours of comradeship. We had a good supper and plenty of whisky but it was all furnished by you boys and I'd like to do a little something for you if you'd accept an old wanderer's meager hospitality."

"You're God damned right we will, Amos," Mike said. "We'd love to be your guests any time anywhere."

"Then, by juckins," Amos says with a flourish, "let's all go up to the wagon and take some medicine."

I started to say something about my health was all right but hadn't more than started when Jimmy kicked me hard on the shin.

"Lead the way, Amos," Jimmy says, "and start uncorking those bottles."

Of course the stuff was pretty mixed up there in the wagon bed and Amos was drunk but he gave everybody a bottle of pills, though I believe Frank did get a bottle of liquid and, yes, so did Jimmy.

Anyway Frank's was some kind of quinine and he went deaf in about an hour. It seems like Jimmy drank a bottle of paregoric which he said turned everything inside him to concrete. But the rest of us boys ate pills and the effects took place quicker. And we had to put poor Oof in the river twice.

But by the third day after that Amos had doctored us up into pretty good shape and said if we were still here when he next passed he'd stop for another supper.

We thought the world of Amos and certainly hated to see him go.

But what I set out to tell was how nice Frank was. For instance when we decided to stock our island with eating animals he let us have a pair of guineas right off. We really had an awful lot in common with him. Old Henderson had never caught Frank stealing anything nor give him any of those hoe-handle whippings but just the same Frank didn't like him. And Frank felt exactly the same way we did about that crooked Newt Tabor up at the store.

But getting back to stocking the island, it all come up this way. We were sitting in camp talking one night about first one thing and then another and drinking a little of that rubbing alcohol Amos had left us when Jimmy said, "Boys, we are laying down on the job."

"We keep the traps baited, don't we?" Mike says.

"Which is true," Jimmy says. "But the Higher Powers have given us two talents. I don't mean like being able to play the trombone, but biblical talents. In other words, business opportunities."

We said what was that and he said our island.

"It grows grass," he said, "for grazing beasts, and bugs for fowls, and roots and grubs for rooting beasts. The Higher Powers fenced it with the river, which can be drunk by animals and that's more than you can say for the finest galvanized barbed wire. In short," he says, "it's just a great big wonderful coop that you don't have to throw feed in because it grows there. But if we don't do something about that talent pretty quick, it will be taken away from us as was always the case in Bible times."

Mike said he didn't see how but even he agreed it would be a fine place to run stock. So as I said, Frank started us off with a pair of pretty speckled guineas. We taxed old man Henderson for three hens and a rooster but Jimmy said it would be disrespectful to try to out-shine the ark, and since two of each kind had replenished the earth, the same number would be a big plenty for Weenie Island, so we said all right and ate the two tenderest-looking hens.

Then Oof came in one day with a little red pig under each arm. And they caused a terrible argument. Frank said they had old Henderson's notch on their ears and Mike said, "Let's just put in more notches and different ones."

But Jimmy said that seemed sneaking to him and think how it would hurt the pigs.

"Let's be men about it," he said. "We won these swine by right of conquest and by God we'll hold 'em the same way."

"Jimmy," I said, "it won't work against a constable."

But Jimmy wouldn't let their ears be renotched, and the thing reached such a deadlock that we finally had to eat them too.

"Anyway," Jimmy said, "we ought to be satisfied with a flock of good mixed poultry like we've got. Our descendants will probably gather tender pullets and little guinea hens and give thanks to their old farsighted sires."

Which was a nice thought, except the hawks caught them right away, all except the guinea rooster. But he couldn't raise unassisted, so the first time we caught him we stewed him, and that was the end of Weenie Island Ranch.

But it wasn't Frank's fault, goodness knows, and when we all got drunk one night and Jimmy said he didn't know what he wouldn't give for some right sad music, Frank went off and got two colored boys name Aleck and Stripes.

Stripes, as you will guess, had had law troubles in the past but was wonderful on that old one-stringed home-made bass fiddle. You'd think it wouldn't work good with just one string, but it did, and this Aleck, who played the French horn and sang, was really an artist.

They said they'd play as much as we could stand up to, for a good mess of fish. Jimmy said that was more than fair and get started, which they did on a piece that went:

Two wheels up
An' two wheels a draggin'
An' you can't ride
In my little waggin.

Jimmy said this was dandy but nowhere near sad enough, so they played "Just Before the Battle, Mother" and went on from there.

The rubbing alcohol was gone but we had two quarts of store whisky and I found three cans of Sterno in an old box we never suspected of holding anything. After the first quart of whisky Jimmy made us drink the Sterno for auld lang syne. I want you to know that by this time we were really in a condition to appreciate each other and what friendship meant.

Finally Mike says, "I feel so wonderful I'll fight any-body in the crowd besides Oof."

Frank said he felt pretty good too and would not let Mike suffer. Frank was sitting on his haunches like farm-ers do, and when Mike started to get up it was just like a lot of wild mules had started kicking him.

That first lick knocked Mike flat and he yelled, "The son of a bitch broke my nose."

Jimmy and Oof and me applauded.

Frank knocked Mike down three times almost before God got the news. But finally Mike got on his feet and did very well. They fought down to the edge of the river and Mike knocked Frank in. It was deep there and every time Frank tried to get out Mike stomped his hands but at last Frank found a shallow place and waded out and beat Mike down to the ground. Frank kicked him about as much as seemed necessary and when Mike got where he couldn't even grunt any more we all agreed that was enough.

Then Oof got his feelings hurt because nobody would fight him. He said he was tired of nothing but lessons and no fun and Jimmy had to let him go boil some fish to get him quiet.

We revived Mike all right, who naturally was full of admiration for Frank now. Me and Jimmy and Oof and the music boys all said how much we enjoyed it and bragged on both of them. But we saw Frank was getting hacked, so Jimmy told Aleck and Stripes to play and we all drank some whisky.

That last quart was about gone when it commenced.

Jimmy said he hated even to mention it, but our friendship was so wonderful, and Frank like a brother to us all, that he just couldn't help it.

"Go ahead," Mike said, who was too drunk to be very sore from his whipping yet. "If there's anything wrong, we want to know about it. Comradeship is precious and we don't want ours getting full of cliques and factions if that's what you mean."

"In a way it is," Jimmy says. "And in a way it ain't. We all have just so many energies and it's natural and what you'd expect that now and then one of those energies would get aimed in the wrong direction."

We said it was and please go on.

"Take a man like Newt Tabor," Jimmy says. "We all know what he is."

"Dishonest," Mike says.

"Yes, and I hope you have had a satisfactory understanding with poor Fanny, his wife. Because there's no doubt but what she needs you."

A smile came on the remains of Mike's face.

"No complaint in that direction," he said. "Everything going fine. And has been for about a week."

"Good," Jimmy says. "But now I will ask you to follow me into something more complex."

We said we'd try.

"Never," he says, "has one of us friends had a wife before. Now, Frank, you will know I mean nothing slurring and wouldn't have you get a divorce for the world. You've got a good-looking wife and we'll just have to figure some way to get around it."

"Thanks," Frank says. "I'm used to her and sort of like her."

"Certainly you do," Jimmy says. "You got there first and took charge and have fed her the corn bread of your own growing. I guess Eddie's the one will have to move over."

"How's that?" I said, surprised.

"We're going to have to ask you to quit pranking with Frank's wife," Jimmy says, "for the simple reason that he's our friend. I know it will mean a sacrifice but it's the only thing to do. And I say this not because of a certain notion you put in her head about me and Mike."

But before I could say anything Frank says, "Eddie, I hate for the thing to come up just this way. I've always figured that, when the time come I couldn't farm a crop of cotton and a crop of corn and keep one woman faithful, I'd get me a tin bill and pick bugs with the chickens. Maybe I'm bragging but I still figure I can do it. But just the same, seeing we're such friends, it might be best if you would lay off Lola, and me make a little trap and catch my own fish."

I jumped up.

"Listen," I said, "I love Frank like a brother but by God that's carrying friendship too far."

"Now, Eddie," Jimmy says, "Frank will forgive you —"

"Forgive hell," I says. "I ain't done anything yet to be forgiven for. Why couldn't you at least give me another week?"

"Friendship won't allow it," Jimmy says. "Besides, there's that woman who herds turkeys. There would be a love affair that would profit us all, had you but eyes to see."

"God damn that old turkey woman," I said. "I don't want nobody but Frank's wife. I've just dwindled away to nothing I want her so bad."

"Eddie," Jimmy says, "we all love you too much to let anything come between us and we'll just have to ask you to swear off of Frank's wife."

"No," I said, "I won't. Nothing you can do can make me."

"Has Oof finished his fish?" Jimmy asked Mike.

Mike said he had.

"Still want to tussle a little," Jimmy asked Oof, "with Eddie maybe?"

Oof jumped up in the air and hollered yes.

So I had to swear off of Frank's wife on my honor as a friend.

Chapter Seven

Y ou can imagine how I felt after they had laid the law down to me about Frank's wife, Lola. I felt just like Moses when he saw Jerusalem but they wouldn't let him in. I had been sure my suit would succeed the next time because I had planned some considerably different tactics. Less talking, that was.

But Jimmy and Mike were just as sympathetic as they could be, and Frank, too, when he wasn't plowing. Then Jimmy had a certain idea and such a lot of things happened that I really didn't have the time for much brooding or even the turkey woman.

Fishing had been awful, and us judge-sober, for about a week. Everybody felt terrible.

Finally Jimmy says, "In a way this bad week has been a blessing."

"Well, maybe I got a shallow mind," Mike said, "but I think you're just plain nuts. Here I am so dry my

69

arms and legs are about to slough off into a powder and you talk about us being blessed."

"I still say so," Jimmy said. "Not a man in this camp has been worse haunted by the sharp brown sweet taste of demon rum than me. I have imagined it burning the throat and simmering on down to the stomach and then exhilarating the nerves and bringing our dried-up souls out of hibernation. I have been a man dying of thirst in a desert and my imagination has poured something like a half a barrel of good red whisky out on the ground before me."

"And you call that a blessing?" I said.

"In a way," Jimmy said. "It has showed me a vision. Necessity just laid down and gave birth to it."

He stopped for a minute to let this sink in.

We kept right quiet.

Then he said, "You know good and well that as long as the fish bit we wouldn't knuckle down and do any real hard sweaty thinking. The Higher Powers saw that the only way they could get us to better ourselves was to cut off the fish and make us unlimber our lazy minds."

All right, we said, and much obliged to the Higher Powers for making us suffer but what was this vision?

"Well," he said, "I envisioned a dark night. There wasn't any light anywhere. Then I stumbled over a bushel basket and when I looked under it there was Oof holding a tallow candle."

"That don't make no sense," Mike said. "Oof can't get under no bushel basket."

"He was standing in a hole," Jimmy says, "and the basket was over the hole. Surely I don't have to explain the meaning of any such simple dream as that."

70

"No," Mike said, "not if you don't mind keeping us in ignorance."

So Jimmy explained it.

What the Higher Powers were trying to put across, he said, was we were just sitting there hiding Oof's light under a bushel. He said when the vision first hit him he couldn't tell right off which light they meant. Then he realized that hole Oof was standing in was more than just a way for the Higher Powers to get Oof under the basket; it was a clue. Otherwise, he said, they'd just have shrunk Oof to fit and gone on about their business. When he had reasoned this far it came over him in a flash and he said he realized then he ought to be bumped for not having seen the whole thing at first.

We said we were tired of waiting and what was it. I think he would have liked to stretch it out longer but he went ahead and said, "The Higher Powers want us to hire Oof out as a well digger."

That was wonderful and we sat there in awe, because well digging is pretty good pay and doesn't take any sense whatsoever.

"All we've got to do," Jimmy says, "is mark a spot on the ground and tell him to dig till he hits water. You boys can draw dirt and, if you want me to, I'll handle the managing end and try to stay tuned in on the Higher Powers for any little suggestions they might want to make."

"Drawing dirt is work," Mike said. "We'll be too worn out to enjoy the fruits of your vision."

But Jimmy promised to hire Aleck and Stripes to draw as soon as business justified it. Not at first,

71

because he meant to name just half of the lowest price ever heard of for well digging so business would be good.

Mike and me felt better about it now and Mike said he wouldn't trade Jimmy for forty Joan of Arcs.

"But first," Jimmy said, "we got to build a clientele."

I said, "Why not start with Newt? All he's got at the store is that old cistern and it full of wiggle tails and the flavor of kerosene."

Besides, Mike said, if we sold him a well it would make it easier to punish him in the future when he got out of line and broke the laws of God or man. We could just drop a few shovelfuls of a certain something in his well, and maybe that would mend his ways.

We went on up to the store and sold Newt a well for twelve dollars. But he wouldn't let us have an advance until we sent Oof back to camp for a shovel and a bucket and a piece of rope and Oof had dug twenty feet of hole. Then he let us have a quart on account. But it went so quick we had Oof run down another twenty feet of hole and in the third twenty, along about daylight, Oof hit water.

We all hollered and romped around because our business was such a success and got the rest of our money in whisky, all except a dollar.

"This dollar," Jimmy says, "goes for bread and baloney and soda pop for our faithful little Oof."

Oof grinned and said that water hole was nothing and he could dig one twice that deep and deeper without straining. He felt so proud and good that he gave us most of his baloney and bread. But we left him the pop and a bite or two of baloney and all went on back

72

to camp happy as so many tired, drunk little larks. We let Oof boil what fish was in the box and then he went to sleep. When the whisky was all gone we did too.

Poor Mike must have been awful drowsy and slept sound, for he rolled over in the fire sometime during the night and slept through the complete burning of one britches leg and a shoe and two and a half toes.

Next day when we woke up we had to laugh because it is Mike who always says Newt's whisky is just rain water and red pepper. However, we put his foot in the tar bucket to keep away the flies and went back to sleep.

That was just the beginning of the well-digging business. When the word got around that our company could run down a well between suns and would do it for just about any price you could name, our business got rushing. We dug four wells that first week.

Mike and me was about dead from drawing dirt. We had two buckets and Oof would shovel dirt in one while we hauled up the other. But no matter how we'd hurry, hoping to get a breathing spell while Oof filled the other bucket, it didn't do us any good. When the empty hit bottom, or maybe his head, he'd just hitch on a full one and holler pull.

We tried to get Jimmy to put Oof back on vegetables but he said nothing doing. I will explain that after the second well Jimmy said we must feed Oof a three-pound baloney ration every day. And then, to cap it all off, Jimmy went to town drunk one day and got to shopping around for something that was strengthening but didn't run into quite so much as baloney, and let somebody sell him twenty-five pounds of dog biscuits.

Mike and me both laughed till we got hysterical like two old women. I think it made Jimmy sort of mad.

He named off a lot of champion foxhounds and two or three bird dogs that the grocer said ate these biscuits.

"Ain't Oof a omnivore just like a dog?" he said.

But we laughed some more and he said, "God damn it, these biscuits got cod-liver oil in 'em, and ground-up bones and plenty of good, strengthening tankage."

He threw a handful to Oof and told him to eat them.

You couldn't have busted one with anything short of a ball-peen hammer, but when Oof clamped down it had to give. It made my jaw ache just to listen to him.

Jimmy said, "They're good, ain't they, Oof?"

Of course Oof said yes, and, if only to save Jimmy's feelings, we quit laughing.

To tell the truth, those dog biscuits did seem to agree with Oof. Sometimes we'd boil them with baloney, or a piece of fat bacon or some fish. But when Oof was well-digging he'd just fill his pockets in the morning and mince along on them dry during the day.

Anyway, after those first few wells, Mike and me was beat down to where the seat of our pants was dragging our tracks out. We called a conference about it.

I said, "Jimmy, we don't want to seem to show the white feather when everything's going along so good financially but Oof's killing us."

"Yes," Mike says. "Why not go on and hire Stripes and Aleck?"

"I just hated to have any outsiders mixed up in our little company," Jimmy says. "I thought you boys would sort of take a pride in it and want to have a hand in its growth. Though if you want to leave it all on me and Oof. . . ."

We do want to keep a hand in its growth," Mike says, "but we ain't going to bust our guts drawing dirt. Hire Aleck and Stripes to draw and me and Eddie will act as your assistants. We've already quit for that matter but we're asking your O.K. of it in the name of auld lang syne."

So Jimmy had to say all right, and hired Aleck and Stripes to draw and I rested hard for about a week.

After that life got to be worth living again. With plenty of time on our hands Mike and me would sit around and talk and wish for things and say what we'd do if we were President of the U.S. Finally we got turkey hungry.

Right there Mike gave us all a shock.

"Let's go steal one," he said.

There was a terrible silence.

"Steal?" Jimmy said.

"Hell yes," Mike said. "I been wanting to steal something for two months. But it's got so, every time I go out and get a little something, you and Eddie go to work on the morals of it and decide it ought to been mine anyway."

"I wish you wouldn't talk that way," Jimmy said. "If you want some turkey meat we'll figure out a legitimate way for you to get it."

"Don't you boys ever have any plain, unvarnished impulses?" Mike said. "I'm just dying to burglarize somebody."

But Jimmy put his foot down.

"Don't people pay the movies millions of dollars for

entertainment?" he says. "Didn't we used to give Stripes and Aleck catfish for entertaining us with music? Of course we did. Therefore music is money."

I remembered we never had bought that garlic.

"Eddie will entertain the turkey woman," Jimmy says, "and Mike can collect a nice young turkey hen for the fee."

"Entertain her how?" Mike says.

"There are certain remarks," Jimmy said, "that no gentleman makes about a lady."

"Well, what's wrong with me?" Mike wanted to know. "I guess I ain't entertaining."

"You've got Fanny," Jimmy says. "And poor Eddie hasn't got anybody since we cut him off from Frank's wife."

Mike said all right, he didn't want to be greedy, but I said, "That's the trouble with you, Jimmy. You're always thinking of others. Why don't you go entertain her yourself?"

"No," Jimmy said. "We'd starve to death for turkey meat if we had to depend on my poor charms."

I argued some more but it didn't do any good.

Me being elected, I waited until the next day when I saw her out herding turkeys and got in the skiff and crossed over. I had an old apple that had been laying around camp for about a week that I meant to give her for a present. Mike didn't come because he said there was no use in him going over there and laying in those bloodweeds and getting full of chiggers until things had got past the preliminary stage.

At the foot of the other bank I tied the skiff and

76

went up a little steep narrow trail. When she saw me coming she picked up a good-sized rock. I stopped about twenty feet away.

She was big but strong looking, not flabby. She had on a pink gingham bonnet and apron. What I could see of her face under the bonnet looked pretty good. It wouldn't win any beauty contests but it wouldn't curdle milk, either.

I said hello and how I had watched her so often from camp and thought neighbors ought to get acquainted. She talked back pretty peaceable and I offered to bring her some catfish sometime but she never did lay down that rock. Finally I said I guessed I'd be going and maybe we'd have another chat before long and she said all right.

I hadn't swept her off her feet but had done very well. I figured that the thickest part of the ice had been broken. But when the time came to give her the apple I got to thinking how good it would taste and just said good-by.

I calculated it would take about three preliminary visits.

On the way home I saw a skiff down at the island and decided I might as well drop down there and see what was going on.

At first I didn't see anybody. I ate a few berries and drank some water. I caught a little snake but hadn't the heart to kill him. Then while I was holding it by the tail, up walked Frank's wife, Lola.

At sight of me she ran and climbed to the first forks of a elm tree.

I sat down right where I'd met her and rolled a cigarette and smoked it. I had started to take a nap when she called had I lost my mind.

I said not that I knew of. I put my hat over my eyes.

"You're just possuming," she said.

"Don't bother me, please," I said. "I want to get some rest."

In a minute I heard the bark rolling and knew she was climbing down the tree.

I just laid there.

"I'm fixing to make a run for my skiff," she said, "and don't you try to catch me."

"I won't," I said.

I waited a minute.

Then I said, "I don't hear nobody running."

"I know your game," she said. "You just want me to come up close so you can grab me."

"That might be it," I said. "You better keep out of reach. Maybe you better just get in that skiff and paddle home. You would certainly be out of harm's way there."

She commenced to cussing me.

The main complaint seemed to be that I was fickle.

I explained to her I had been communing with my conscience and decided it would not be honorable to prank with my friend Frank's wife.

"You mean," she says, "you're going to let a little old fishhook acquaintanceship stand between you and your heart's desire?"

I said I guessed that was about the size of it and turned over on my stomach.

I couldn't help but laugh to myself when I heard her switch off to the skiff. After a minute I heard her come back walking slow. I lay right quiet.

Suddenly something heavy hit me first across the shoulders, next across the legs, then over the head and just about everywhere else.

When I came to I felt like every bone in my body was crushed. I must have laid there thirty minutes before I could get to the skiff. When I finally did, it was torture rowing back to camp.

The boys met me and helped me out and wanted to know how come me so bloody. I told them I had found two baby panthers on the island and started to the skiff with them when a grown one jumped me.

I knew that was terrible but I was half out of my head and couldn't think of anything better.

Mike and Jimmy started laughing.

I got mad.

"What the hell's so funny?" I said.

Mike said, "Oh, not nothing, only I never heard of a panther beating anybody up without scratching them. I guess this one wore boxing gloves."

I was nearly dead anyway, and now this had to happen.

I told them what really took place on the island, and Mike rolled on the ground laughing and said that was the biggest lie he ever heard in his life. He said it would be an insult to his and Jimmy's intelligence if it wasn't so funny.

I ran for the shotgun. But Jimmy beat me to the shells and Oof and Mike tied me up.

They gave me a drink out of a quart they had just bought and promised to believe me and not tell Frank.

I said all right, I wouldn't kill Mike and they untied me but all I can say is, it's a good thing Jimmy kept those cartridges in his pocket.

79

Things went on just fine and prosperous as you please with no especial difficulties for another week or so. Our well-digging crew was making the dirt fly and the money was rolling in so fast we hardly ever drew a sober breath any more. Sometimes Jimmy and me would go to the store in the middle of the night for whisky and cheese and stay there talking with Newt for forty or fifty minutes.

"Where is Mike?" Newt would say.

"Off playing a prank on somebody," we'd say.

Then Newt would laugh and say, "Who?"

"We promised not to tell," we'd say.

Once we heard some footsteps upstairs that didn't sound very feminine. Newt looked worried but of course he didn't dare go off and leave us down in the store for fear we'd get an extra nibble of cheese or something.

But on this same night we had hardly quieted Newt down from hearing the footsteps when there came an awful whack against the ceiling. Most anything could have made that noise but it just seemed more likely to believe it was a bed slat. Anyway Newt covered up as much stuff as he could and grabbed his six-shooter and started running up the steps.

I was scared as I could be.

I guess Jimmy saw it.

"After all, nobody ain't dead yet," he says. "Newt is making a lot of fuss getting up the steps."

We heard something heavy hit the ground hard outside the window. Upstairs Newt ran to the window and took four quick shots with that .38.

Jimmy said he was glad it was such a dark night.

"One of those soft-nosed .38s goes in little," I said, gloomy, "but it comes out big as a cup bottom."

In a minute Newt came faunching down the steps.

"What's the trouble?" we said.

"A Mexican slipped up the back stairs and tried to burglarize Fanny. But I plugged the son of a bitch," Newt said, tickled. "He won't bust into nair 'nother honest man's home."

He got his flashlight and we went outside.

We found blood where Newt said he shot him and followed it about fifty feet to a bush. Jimmy gulped and I crossed myself. We walked around the bush. There, stone dead with a bullet-busted skull, lay Newt's milk cow.

We didn't dare laugh while Newt was holding that six-shooter. Later, Jimmy said he really hoped nothing would ever come any closer to rupturing him.

When Newt finally quit cussing the Mexican and that poor cow for getting in the way, he tried to get us to help dress the carcass. We said we'd love to help him but we had to get some rest for tomorrow's well-digging. He said he'd give us a whole forequarter and half the liver. I said grass-fed beef was just tough and flabby and Jimmy said he could never eat beef killed by a bullet intended for a human, Mexican burglar or not.

We went on back to the store, us to get our purchases and Newt his butcher knife and whetrock. Then we discovered this bad Mexican must have run under the house instead of away, because somebody had stole a case of beer and a block of hard chili and twenty pounds of ice and several big pocketfuls of sardines and chewing tobacco.

We said this was certainly a pity, and good night, and we hoped those Mexicans would leave him alone in the future.

Back at camp we found Mike red-rooster proud of having turned an ambush into a biblical talent. He had already drunk three bottles hot and had the rest cooling, and Oof, who had give up trying to figure out what the little key was for, was opening sardines with his teeth, just catching that tab of leftover tin and pulling up.

Chapter Eight

A long about here a little out-of-the-ordinary something came up concerning Oof.

You just let a few people learn you can start a well in the morning and be drinking water out of it that night and the news will travel pretty fast. Especially if you are a sort of savage and about seven feet tall and have two as big liars as Aleck and Stripes drawing dirt for you. They were good boys but just didn't seem able to stand up against their imagination.

We were pretty sure they were the ones who started it that Oof could eat a whole shoat at a sitting and liked it better if it wasn't cooked. Also that he could bend a railroad rail with his hands and feet and split kindling with his head. I know it was them said that when Oof shook the rope signaling them to haul up, that if they had hold of it, all four of their feet flew off the ground.

Of course Oof wasn't quite such a man as this but

Jimmy said never mind denying these rumors because they stimulated the well-digging business.

Privately Mike and me decided Jimmy was too proud of what he called Oof's legend to tell the truth, which would have been hard enough to believe, be known. For instance those dog biscuits, which Jimmy still bought for Oof, showed you that he was about Oof like some men are about trotting horses or high-bred poultry. We never mentioned it but the truth was, Jimmy got to be kind of a cannibal fancier.

Anyway this reputation of Oof's had its troublesome side like everything else. The colored girls and women, taking for granted Oof was a Negro too, as he very well might have been for all anybody knew, did their best to make a fool out of him. Whenever we'd pass they'd make eyes at him and titter. Every now and then one would run up to him with a pencil and a piece of paper and ask him to autograph it. He'd grab the pencil and write + which was his mark. Then the rest would swoop down and want their papers marked too.

Occasionally Oof would snatch up one of the more choice ones and try to run to cover with her but we always stopped him and would try to calm him down by reasoning with him.

We said the way his fame was growing, it would hit Africa before long and some African princess, maybe several, would get in a ship and come after him because princesses had to have the best of everything. In Africa he would be the big boss, we said, with eight pairs of red silk britches. He would have three flunkeys boiling fish all day long, and molasses candy till he busted.

Finally we got where we sort of believed it ourselves

and would say, "Now wouldn't it be funny if all of this just hauled off and came true?"

Just in case it did, Jimmy volunteered for Prime Minister and Mike said he would act as foreman of the harem if we couldn't get anybody else. I said just give me a job in the post office and a good basket of lunch to take to work every day. I'd sit around and read what postcards came in and pass the time of day with the stamp buyers.

But on our trips to town we had almost more trouble with the Negro boys than the girls because every time one got good and drunk he would try to jump on Oof. They knew they'd get whipped pretty bad but I guess they figured it wouldn't hurt much drunk. If they lived through it they could say they had had the nerve to jump on that wild man who could whip anybody in the world.

After one or two of these little spats we tried to leave Oof at home when we went to town. But he'd follow us, hiding behind bushes like a dog, until finally I got sorry for him.

"Let's tie his hands behind him with the skiff chain," I said, "and let him come on."

We did, and that very day a big Negro jumped on Oof in town and commenced to whipping him with a fence picket. Eventually I guess he would have hurt Oof if Oof hadn't ducked his head and butted the Negro in the face, de-nosing him. Oof butted him twice in the stomach and both times you could hear the ribs crack.

After that, besides tying Oof's hands, we put a rope on his neck with a slip knot in it so all of us could set back against it and choke him down.

85

However, the constable caught us one day and wanted to put us in jail for holding Oof in peonage with ropes. But Oof explained it was necessary because otherwise a lot of useful farm labor might get destroyed. I think this made the constable sort of mad. He said if Oof hadn't any better sense than to like it, lead him on down the street, and we did.

That same day we met some Negro boys in a wagon who asked if they could take Oof home with them to dig a well. They promised not to get him on a rampage and to have him back safe and sound the next night.

"No," Jimmy says. "You better go along, Eddie, and keep things regular."

When we got there about daylight they led me to the corncrib where they gave me a cup and a stool and showed me a barrel of dewberry wine with a spigot in it. I told Oof to go dig these nice colored folks a well.

After that I seem to have sort of lost track of time. The next I knew Oof was wearing a strange hat and dipping wine out of the top of the barrel with a sirup bucket and drinking it. He said a day and night had passed since I came into the crib.

I will try to tell you what happened. But first I have got to go into the nature of this bunch of Negroes. There were nine boys and one girl in this outfit, and the girl ruled the roost. The whole bunch was Holy Rollers but the girl could outroll and outholler most anybody.

Her name was Delilah. And she had took up the notion she was the same Delilah out of the Bible. When she heard about Oof she decided he was Samson and told her brothers to go hire a well dug.

So, as you know, they hauled us out there in the wagon and beguiled me with dewberry wine.

Anyway they took Oof on the porch and made him acquainted with Delilah. She sent the brothers off squirrel hunting and took him in the parlor where she tried to tell him he was Samson. But Oof said no he wasn't.

When she told him how strong Samson was Oof said give him a good spade and Stripes and Aleck to draw and he'd outdig this Samson any day in the week.

I guess she saw he never would catch on to what she meant.

"Well, let's just go on and get married anyway," she said.

Oof said he was waiting for an African princess.

"What do you think I am?" she says. "We've got three hundred acres of good mesquite land. Those brothers of mine are my army when I'm mad and my flunkeys when I'm not. And unless you're color blind, you ought to could tell I had African ancestors."

Oof said she didn't seem like much princess to him. Besides, he told her, she was sin-ugly and he came here to dig a well.

I'm sure this made her mad but she held in till her brothers got back and told them to get Oof drunk. Which they did.

It was the next day before Oof woke up. He said when he did he felt funny right off. Then he went to scratch his head and found out something was missing.

They were all standing around looking at him and, I guess, laughing at the poor bald-headed thing. Delilah held up the shears and said they were her sign over him and now he was her slave.

Oof said that was a hell of a way to treat company but he'd go on and make the best of it.

"I guess you will, you onion-headed weakling," Delilah said. "From now on, when I say froggy, you jump."

"You no want well dug?" Oof said, catching on. "You just want Oof's hair?"

They said that was right.

"Oof want his hair back," Oof said. "That all the hair Oof had."

He said would they please give it to him in a paper sack and tell him where I was and let him go home.

They said no.

"Please," Oof said. "Oof no want to make knock-knock."

They all laughed at him for talking as big as if he still had his hair. Oof told me this hurt his feelings.

He caught the two that were closest to the bed and popped their heads together and dropped them on the floor.

He said he still was not mad but just wanted to end this talk about him being a weakling.

He said naturally he hated to lose his hair but people got such strange ideas in this country, and half the time meant no real harm, that he intended to let the matter drop. He just wanted to find me and go on back to camp and rub a certain something on his head which poor Oof thought would make hair grow since it was such a wonderful help to a vegetable garden.

But anyway one of the brothers got excited and shot

Oof in the leg with a derringer. Maybe this one hadn't meant no harm either, Oof said, but he had certainly done some. Oof said he guessed he was just a high-tempered savage but that bullet stung and he got mad and took in after them.

Oof said since they had taken such pains to teach him about their God he got a real enjoyment out of making them acquainted with his.

After he had a couple of buckets of that good berry wine I made him take me where he'd left each one to see that they were all still breathing. Happily they were.

We felt pretty good and went on back to the house and cooked some pork sausage and drank a little wine. We filled a couple of gallon jugs and picked up a few souvenirs at the smokehouse and started back to camp.

On the way home I gave Oof a handful of hair I'd found in a currycomb and he was tickled to death, though he said he had never known his was quite that shade before.

Oof's part of the thing was finished now but mine hadn't begun. I told him to say he found me tied to that barrel by a strong rope. He said he would. He said he would do anything for little Eddie and, just to prove it, gave me back a few strands of that roan hair for a keepsake.

Chapter Nine

Back at camp, of course I had to hear remarks about sending a boy to the mill and how worried they'd been, and it looked like if you wanted anything done right you had to do it yourself, and in the future they guessed they'd have to trail Oof everywhere he went, even to the ditch. In the meantime we had fished the bullet out of Oof's leg with an ice pick and kerosened it and tarred it and tied it up with a rag.

I fried some ham and heated a jar of that ash hominy and said if they didn't mind accepting the hospitality of an idiot, come and get it.

I sent Oof up to the road where we'd hid the wine in some bushes and after we'd drunk about a gallon Jimmy says, "Show me the man who is so perfect he never makes mistakes."

Mike said he wouldn't like him if he knew him.

I guess the wind must have been blowing toward

Frank's house, for in a minute here he came with a pocketful of Gray Dove biscuits and an appetite you could have hung a saddle on.

They all bragged on the ham and hominy and said a little dewberry wine was wonderful for a change.

Then Frank said he wanted to thank me for the way I kept my word over on the island the other day, and Mike snickered.

"Don't laugh," Frank said. "For I know it's true."

"I just thought of something funny," Mike said, "something that didn't have anything to do with that."

"I love you, Mike," Frank said, "but you're a God damn liar. You laughed because Eddie came in showing the signs of that beating Lola gave him with a skiff paddle."

"Even if I did," Mike said, reaching for the iron skillet, "you ain't man enough to make me admit it."

"I never thought the time would come," Jimmy says, "when our friends and guests couldn't come to this camp and have discourse without certain ones of us wanting to give them a skillet whipping."

"Me either," I said, playing disgusted.

Mike got mad and threw the skillet in the river.

"All right," he said. "That's what I was laughing at."

He sat down and tried to let on he wasn't ashamed.

"Please proceed," Jimmy says to Frank. "If you've discovered the least bit of truthfulness in Eddie I am mighty interested in hearing about it."

"There's nothing to it," Frank said. "Only Lola came home and said she beat Eddie up with a boat oar and I says what for, in the name of peace?

92

"'Because he insulted me and is as fickle as the day is long,' she said.

"'How did he insult you, baby doll?' I said.

"And she said, 'He just did, that's all.'

"So I meant to come down here before long and thank Eddie because maybe I am not the brainiest somebody in the world but I could pretty well picture what insulted her. However, when I smelled that ham cooking I decided now was as good a time as any."

In about ten minutes I had rose from being a skunk and a mill-sent boy to sort of a hero. Jimmy said I ought to be in the schoolbooks because my honesty had prevailed before the fact instead of only afterwards when the tree was dead, like George Washington.

"And if you think it's easy," he says, "just ask our tried and true Eddie."

I said of course it was hard but what was life without honor.

Mike said I ought to get a medal because every time he thought of Lola himself his mouth watered.

When we finished the second jug Jimmy said he'd been jotting down a little verse to fit the occasion but wouldn't bother us by reading it out loud. So we made him read it.

This was the piece:

"Blessed is Eddie, in the bonds our friend,
Who wines us and dines us till we can't bend.
What if he let Oof's leg get punctured with a tiny piece of lead?
Oof ain't dead.
But telling the truth is where Eddie shines mainly.

93

For after chasing Frank's wife, Lola, about forty miles
vainly,
   And we said desist,
   Did he resist?
   Well, naturally some, but just the same
   When it was that or fight Oof Eddie was game
   And said, 'I'd nearly as soon in that old river drown
   But since it's in friendship's sweet name I will take my
sign down.'

   "And then, by God, where she'd always run,
   Lola turned and chased this friendly one
   And when she had him on an island hemmed
   And saw his zeal for honesty could not be stemmed
   She lambasted poor Eddie with a rowboat paddle
   Till pain overcame him and his wits began to addle
   But true was our dear Eddie to his ideal
   And he didn't give in when his head she peeled.

   So here's to Eddie, a man in full,
   Three feet wide and made all of wool.
   We love him, by God, for the true friend he is
   And how he resisted Frank's hell-bent Mrs."

A silence fell. Finally Frank said he had never read
any printed poetry that was better than that and I was
dying to say, "I guess not because you couldn't read
your own name."

But Mike sniffled and since it was written to me I
thought I'd better cry a little too and did. After we'd all
bragged the best we could Jimmy said it wasn't much
but he was glad it suited our simple tastes. Then Frank

94

got up to go home but staggered off in the wrong direction so Jimmy sent Oof to lead him and we turned in.

But shot or no shot, Oof managed to limp down a couple of wells that week and, I think, three the next, so we really were not in want and struggled along pretty well, including me and the turkey woman. But before this goes any further, please understand you mustn't expect too much from this turkey-woman romance. As I have said, she was not just mud-ugly or defective in any way. But we all know it takes a little more than not having anything especially wrong with you to make romance quiver and flame. For instance the way some women walk gets me mighty romantic. I remember Conchita. When she walked, something happened to you. And Frank's wife, Lola, had it too, till her cup ran over. But the turkey woman didn't. Whenever I saw her, my mind ran to roast turkey and that's about all.

Just the same I tried to be conscientious. On my second visit she found out we'd been to Hollywood and commenced to bombard me with questions about movie stars. Half of them I'd never heard of but I answered everything the way I thought she wanted it and tried, at the same time, to work in the romantic note just the least bit.

She stood hitched very well and made no objection to this slightly sentimental turn things had taken. When I left she wanted to know when I was coming back. I said in a day or two and when I got back to camp I told Mike he'd better be ready to pick up a turkey on my next visit.

But there were such a lot of pretty interesting things happened along in here that I will leave the turkey woman herding her flock for a while and come back to her, according to schedule, day after tomorrow or the next day. For Frank had butchered a shoat that same afternoon and traded ham and a forequarter to Newt for a half gallon of whisky.

All this ran counter to Frank's plans, which had been to kill a yearling. However, when he had gone to arrange his trade with Newt beforehand, Newt had said he not only would not give Frank any whisky for that yearling meat but would not let it come on the place free of charge.

He said Fanny and him had both gone nearly beef-crazy already from gnawing on that old milk cow. None of the markets would buy her because she was grass fed. Of course Newt had been too stingy to give any of it away so he and, mainly I guess, poor Fanny had had to eat the whole carcass unassisted. When they got down to the last forequarter Newt came in and found a note saying Fanny had run off with a baking-powder salesman. She said she didn't know where she was going except away from him and the last quarter of that old tough beef, though she was no more tired of it than she was of him.

I guess Newt was glad to get rid of her, for I suppose keeping a woman is an expense. But it cut Mike to the quick, and he took up the shotgun to go to the store and kill Newt.

"The idea," he says, looking for the shells which happily Jimmy had in his pocket, "of that rock-hearted son of a bitch making that girl devour that old canner cow, though I doubt if it was even fit to be canned."

But we stopped him and Frank dressed the shoat, since Newt didn't care for any of the yearling, and got the whisky. We baked the spareribs and backbone and a few strings of sausage down at the camp.

These roasted pork bones were wonderful but we were all sad on Mike's account, for he could hardly take a drink without wanting to go slay Newt.

But Jimmy says, "Bear up strong, little bereaved friend, under the yoke that wicked bastard of a Newt has buckled on your neck. The Higher Powers grind slow but they grind mighty fine. Which means that in the end they will fix Old Newt and in all probability do it in a way to benefit the righteous."

I said, "Mike, just as soon as we get the edge off our turkey appetite, seeing as I started it and we'd lose time if I didn't go ahead and get the first turkey, you can have the turkey woman."

Mike said much obliged for the sentiment and the turkey woman but he wanted Fanny back.

Of course we didn't even know where she was and couldn't get her back for him but Jimmy, always thoughtful and tender around those with a battered heart, says, "I just wish we weren't so powerless in the face of destiny but, if you think it'd cheer you up any, I'd be mighty glad to arrange for you to give old Henderson one of those fence-jumping whippings."

Now in spite of a crushed heart, Mike couldn't help grinning. For the first time tonight he bit off a piece of pork. It was wonderful to see him taking an interest in things again.

"It wouldn't make me feel so good," Mike said, "if he'd just whipped me for stealing milk and vegetables. But mostly he done it for fun. And while that's all right too, I don't see why I ain't entitled to the same kind of fun."

We said by all means he was, and all went to the spring looking for a nice weight and size of willow limb and found one. Then we came on back and ate pork and drank whisky till just before day, when we caught and tied old Henderson's heifer in the corner of the fence.

Pretty soon here he come, mad, talking to himself about boys playing pranks but he certainly tanned one milk-stealer's hind end in this very corner and he bet it was stinging yet and he had to laugh when he thought about it.

We had tied a hard knot in the rope where it went on the fence but a bowknot on the cow, so while old Henderson was fiddling with the hard knot Mike untied the bow and held the rope and pushed the cow away.

We were out of sight.

Finally old Henderson got his end untied and turned around.

"Morning, Mr. Henderson," Mike says.

Mr. Henderson tried to say something but hadn't any luck.

"I was just wondering," Mike says, "if you could put on the same kind of dance as I did if I sort of helped you with this green willow limb."

"But I caught you stealing milk," old Henderson says.

"Well, if you think that helped cool off my behind from that hoe handle," Mike says, "you're mistaken."

Which seemed to me like something to think about.

Finally Mike jumped him through the wires and we went on home to get ready for the constable. Which didn't amount to any more than Mike spending the day on Weenie Island and Oof going after him in the skiff when the constable was gone.

On the appointed day I went back to court the turkey woman and did first rate, I guess, because when I got back to the skiff Mike was waiting with a nice spring hen.

On the way home, however, I said, "I promised you my interest in the turkey woman, Mike, but she has romantic qualities a little beyond my expectations. I don't think there's any question about her not having affection enough for both of us. So if it's all right with you, let's just go halvers."

That suited Mike fine and I skinned the turkey while he rowed across to camp.

Chapter Ten

There was right smart talk about the Hackberry Fair which was to come off soon.

"I heard some of them say there was going to be a turtle race," Mike said, unluckily, "and a grand prize of two dollars and a half to the winner."

"Do you reckon anybody in these parts breeds racing turtles?" Jimmy said.

We said our guess was no.

"Well, I'm not lured by that measly little purse," Jimmy says, "but the idea of a turtle race sort of touches off my imagination."

He said he'd always wanted a string of racing horses but the Higher Powers had never seen fit to let him have them.

"Yet God knows they have certainly flooded us with turtles," he said. "And, after all, that two and a half would buy a quart of whisky for the victory celebration."

We said hurrah for us having already won the race with a turtle we didn't even have, but how had we managed it?

"Because," Jimmy says, "other folks will just catch a turtle and hope he wins. We'll train ours."

Mike and me was pretty cold toward running a turtle stable but Jimmy couldn't talk of anything else.

So I had to go to town next day for a quarter's worth of beef heart, which is good turtle bait, and commence fishing for turtles, which I hate the sight of anyway.

Of course Jimmy said the first one we caught was heavensent and bragged on its strong hind legs and trim low-slung build which would be such a help in taking fast corners.

As I remarked, I hate turtles. This one especially. He had wide jaws and a little smart-Alecky turned-up chin and a look in his eyes that gave you to understand he figured he had more sense than you did, which is a hard thing to stand in anybody.

Anyhow we put him in a tub and all tried to think up a name for him. Mike said since Jimmy had read so many books, why didn't he rack his brains for something literary? Jimmy said he had read such a few books on turtles he was at a loss unless we would be satisfied with just working out the Fair angle.

We said anything, just so he gets a name.

He said, "Well, a fellow named Thackeray wrote a book once called *Vanity Fair* —"

"Don't go no further," Mike said. "You'd never find a better turtle name in a million years."

102

That suited Oof and me, so we named him W. M. Thackeray and commenced trying to teach him to run.

We'd tie a piece of meat on a string and trail it in front of him. At first he wouldn't try very hard but we put him on such a strict diet that he finally got where he'd take a real interest in his practice. As soon as he'd break into a lope we'd let him have some meat.

Mike and me took mighty little stock in the whole thing besides just what little was forced on us by politeness.

"Have patience," Jimmy said, "and faith. After all, W. M. Thackeray will not be running against greyhounds but just some old country turtles with nothing like his training."

However, it was a strain even on Jimmy because that turtle flatly refused to take Jimmy into his heart.

I had always said there was no good in a turtle. God just make them to plague mankind the same as he did lice and poison ivy.

But Jimmy said now his pride was involved and he'd win W. M. over if it cost every cent we could rake and scrape for beef heart.

Lots of times when Jimmy wasn't there Mike and me would cuss W. M. and say he was breaking Jimmy's heart. Do you think it did any good? Not one bit. He'd just look at us like ain't you crazy and tiresome. Then he'd pull in his head to avoid our company.

But even if he was mean, the old devil finally got where he could run pretty good. These days we would let him out of the tub for a swim because it was awful hot. We kept a string on his leg while he had his bath and would tie him to a stick when he got out.

Had everything gone on as planned, I guess W. M. would have carried off the honors at the Fair.

Like I said, it was hot weather and half the time we laid around in the shade of the bridge with no clothes on. One day Mike and me went off to town and left Jimmy taking his ease with nothing on, and that cussed W. M. Thackeray tied out on a string.

We never discussed what happened to poor Jimmy while he was taking his innocent nap there in the shade. All I know is we found him in misery and I ran to the store for some salve.

Newt wanted to know what was wrong.

"That damn snapping turtle," I said. "He's done one of the most ungrateful things I ever heard of."

He wanted all the details. I told him what little I knew.

Well, Newt had just little enough sympathy for suffering humanity to run through the door, screen and all, and fall on the porch laughing.

After it was all over Mike and me never made the slightest reference to the late W. M. Thackeray in Jimmy's poor wounded presence. Though we did have a chuckle or two on the side.

Anyway we had turtle soup for supper that night but Jimmy said if we didn't mind, just fry him a few slices of bacon.

It actually looked like the Higher Powers had got mad at us. We hadn't done a thing. But it certainly looked that way. Right on the heels of that lowdown trick W. M. played on Jimmy, Oof had his little accident.

He was digging a well and had got down thirty or

forty feet when the hauling rope broke and dropped a bucket of dirt on his head. It would have killed anybody else double-dead that minute but Aleck ran for another rope and when Stripes let him down he found Oof still breathing. Aleck said the weight of that bucket hitting his head had drove Oof's feet down in the clay about six inches and he guessed if Oof had been standing on a rock it would have broke both legs.

Anyway they drew him out and laid him across Aleck's mule and brought him on into camp. It looked like he was going to stay unconscious forever, though I guess he was having a good time because all he did was give orders to the court and the army and send a boy to see if the princess was sleepy and order candy and fish and fried bacon.

We were all terribly put out about it and laid the blame on Stripes and Aleck for not having told us, except three times, that the rope was worn out. They said they were sorry and would try to do better in the future if Oof's digging days weren't forever ended.

I'll tell you we were kind of lost without him because there was nobody to paddle the skiff or get up wood or wash the dishes or any of those little duties that Oof always did when he got home from work.

"It's funny how blind you can be," Mike says, "to the goodness of your loved ones when they are sound in body and right there under foot."

That got us started and Jimmy made some mighty pretty remarks. I guess he quoted the Bible, for he says, "Blessed is he who diggeth holes in the dry earth and bringeth forth good well water to the parched lips of his brethren."

"I never knew before how much good could rest in a heathen," Mike said, sad.

I said poor Oof was just as handy as a pocket in a shirt.

But Mike said even though we were cut out of our well-digging money, Oof was no expense to us whatever because even Oof couldn't eat unconscious and it was restful to be able to go to town knowing he could not get into anything.

Jimmy said he guessed that was the silver lining to a mighty bad cloud and maybe Mike and me ought to step down to the skiff and look in the fish traps. He said he would keep a vigil beside our little slap-happy friend.

I was really glad somebody had remembered the traps, which are just like having money out at interest.

"You reckon the fish are all dead?" Mike said.

"I don't see why they should be," I said. "There's plenty of good river water runs through those traps and the fish ought not to be too high-toned to eat rotten corn since that's what they went in there for."

Mike said maybe they would still be alive but did I figure the meat would be any better and firmer on a corn-fed catfish than on a just ordinary one?

I said I didn't see why not; it was true of hogs and cows and country girls.

"Then why oughtn't we charge Newt extra for 'em?" he wanted to know.

"No use," I said. "Newt will crook us out of that extra value because he is the kind of man who would steal the Lord's supper and do a certain disgraceful something with the tablecloth."

"Anyway," Mike says, "it's nice to be fishing again

and wondering what kind of catch you will make instead of knowing beforehand what you will get from a well."

"Me too," I said. "I been nearly stifled with all this security."

Something had happened to the first two traps. Somebody either stole them or they had washed away. But the third one was still there. I tried to pull it up.

"What's the matter?" Mike says.

"Buried in the mud," I said.

I gave another pull and it moved the least bit. Finally we got it to the bank and pulled out the God-awfullest chicken coopful of catfish you ever saw. They were wedged in there like sardines.

When we spread them out in the skiff there was no place for us to sit without getting finned, so we led the boat down the sand bar and on into camp.

We had to go get Frank to hitch up Pud and Eagle to haul them to the store.

Then after all the trouble we'd gone to, Newt said he could never handle that many fish at ten cents a pound until Mike said, "Just go on and don't buy 'em. I've been waiting a long time for an admittable excuse to whip your ears off, and if you turn down these fish, that's it."

Frank knew where Newt kept his gun and leaned back against the drawer and wouldn't let Newt have it.

So we got twenty-three dollars for our fish. We bought eight quarts of whisky and the ham Frank had traded Newt and some bread and onions. We also got a quarter's worth of ice to set on Oof's head to see if that would make him come to.

Back at camp we got fixed nice and comfortable and set out to drink our whisky. First Jimmy made us a good long talk on the insides of crawfish, which he said scientists spoke of as "crayfish."

Mike said that was what he hated about scientists: they wouldn't just go on and call a thing by its right name but had to give everything a nickname in Greek and Hindu so their talk would pass over other people's heads and they could get by with wearing chin whiskers.

Jimmy said he wouldn't argue about it but anyway a crawfish had two stomachs and a set of teeth separating them that chewed food automatically like an electric coffee grinder ground coffee.

From there we went to inflation, which Jimmy said was one of the burning questions of the day. If we didn't look out, he said, our fish money would get where it was worthless.

This scared Mike and me both. Mike said he'd taken just about all he was going to take off of old Franklin Roosevelt, what with the way the Relief had treated us in California.

"And now," Mike says, "he means to take the goody out of our little fish money."

I said maybe he would come to his senses eventually.

"Why, God damn him," Mike says, "he don't do nothing but sit up there and crack jokes over the radio and lay his own meanness off on somebody else."

Jimmy said if Oof ever got well we'd probably get rich. Yet what good would it do us?

"He'll tax us out of every cent of it," Jimmy says, "to pay for his foolhardiness."

Of course that settled it. We all took the Republican

oath on the spot and said we'd electioneer for a yellow dog before we would vote for that wastrel of a Roosevelt who was spending our money faster than Oof could make it.

Then, since we were mad anyhow, we got off on old Hitler. Finally we worked ourselves up to where we had to write him a letter to keep from busting.

It was really a masterpiece. It was one of the most scientific and literary pieces you ever read and, I reckon, one of the dirtiest.

But Mike said it hadn't worked off half of his indignation and made me get up and fight.

I don't think there was any question but he'd have killed me if a miracle hadn't happened.

Oof opened his eyes.

We all yelled glory hallelujah and quit our spat to start looking for any wagon-spilt fish along the road, since Oof said he was famished.

There were several wells on the docket to be dug, so while Oof ate we said, "If your little sickness has got you down and you are no longer the great well digger you used to be and don't mind losing your reputation, just let them go until some other time."

He insisted on starting at once whether he felt like it or not.

"You understand we are not hurrying you," we said, "because it is not our reputation that is at stake; no women follow us around wanting our autograph, nor would an African princess have us on a bet."

But he was determined, so we said, "Go get Stripes and Aleck and take back four pounds of bacon and swap it for a new piece of rope."

Maybe you've never had one and don't know but there is nothing that rids a man's mind of the shoddy financial details of life like a good steady income. At the same time, nothing is worse than to have somebody who is supposed to be a worker sitting around doing nothing whether he is unconscious or not. When you've got them there idle it's like having money you're not supposed to spend, or a lackluster lady friend, or like old Hitler having all that army and can't get anybody to have a war with. Some folks, like Jimmy for instance, you don't expect any work from and it would worry you to see them doing it, but to have Oof sitting around idle is like having a bush that won't grow.

We all felt worlds better being back in the money and talked about what it did for your morale.

Since Frank's crop was laid by, he didn't have any demands on his time and there was really not a whole lot we had to do besides just sit there and every once in a while open our mouths and swallow.

Then here came a boy saying the sheriff had his papa, Mexican Pete. They lived down the river a piece in a sort of cave dug in the side of an old lignite coal-mine dump. The boy said the sheriff caught Pete raising marijuana and had already pulled about three thousand dollars worth and loaded it on his car. He also said his poor Mamacita was worried nearly to death because with Pete in jail they'd starve, and starving really amounted to something when there was nothing in your cigarette but Bull Durham.

This sort of revived us all.

Jimmy said if Pete had been growing junk around

here we'd certainly been cheated out of our little occasional pinch or two as neighbors. But just the same, he'd go have a talk with the sheriff about what a good husband and father Pete was. Jimmy also said if anything happened to the weeds while this talk went on it would be hard to convict Pete on just the sheriff's say-so.

So while Jimmy went down to Pete's cave and talked to the sheriff we carried all the marijuana to the river and threw it in. There was a lot of good thick underbrush between the road and the cave so we stepped back to the car and got the seat cushions and rugs and tires and a good wide strip of oilcloth off the top. We also found a ten-gallon copper kettle in the back which had once been part of a still, I guess, and filled it nearly full with what gasoline was in the tank.

We had buried these items on Weenie Island and been back to camp about an hour when Jimmy came in.

"If you ain't the most capricious boys," he says. "When that poor sheriff came out and looked at that car, it came in an inch of salivating him."

"My motto," Mike says, "is be helpful: help those that are looking for trouble to find it."

Then Jimmy saw Oof and says, "What on earth happened to Oof's caboose?"

"Don't notice it," I said. "God knows what he wants with it but he pulled off the steering wheel and hid it in the seat of his pants."

Oof said he wanted it for a swing seat to ride up and down wells when he was tired so he wouldn't have to hold on to the rope.

We all complimented him on his foresight but Jimmy

said the sheriff had promised Pete five dollars and all charges dropped if he could get his stuff back and not tell anybody, because it was just two weeks before election time.

We said we would, providing Pete promised not to grow any more junk, which anybody knows deadens the senses and makes tramps out of good men. If we caught him at it again, we said, we'd turn Oof loose on him. Also, we said, have him tell that sheriff that the Brazos Forks neighborhood takes care of its own, that there are forces at work which will nip any iniquity in the bud and will do the same for nosy sheriffs. We said for Pete to tell this sheriff he would get one of our Sunday pillagings next time, instead of any such little halfhearted borrowing as took place today.

So that night Pete showed the sheriff a note that had been thrown against the cave front tied on a rock. It said his stuff was buried on the island and told where. All except the steering wheel, which, it said, he could tell the voters fell off and got lost.

By noon the next day the car was gone. We all felt wonderful about this little skirmish with the law and how well it turned out. Pete said he was a changed man and sent us a bucket of chili made of swamp-rabbit meat for our trouble.

That night we saw him put a letter in the tin mailbox by the bridge.

I went over and got it and read it. It was to somebody in San Antonio ordering more marijuana seeds on credit. He said he'd be plenty able to pay for them because this time he would plant on Weenie Island and if the weeds were found everybody would think they

112

belonged to three fishermen that lived under the bridge.

Next night we bumped into Pete down on the island where he was getting his ground ready. Mike and me cut a couple of good stout willow limbs. Jimmy took Oof, who might have been hard to stop at the right time, on back to the skiff and waited for us.

We were not mad at Pete, just a little disappointed. We told him we believed there was a smattering of good in him and only meant to beat the bad out. After about half an hour I think we had.

During the month that followed this little paddling Pete was not the spriest somebody in the world but by the end of the second one he got a job as a section hand and lived the life of a useful citizen.

Now that the Pete incident was finished and there was time to give a little thought to our own business, Jimmy called a meeting.

"Boys," he said, "I know how Newt must have felt after gnawing on that old cow for the first three weeks."

We knew what he meant but didn't say anything because we figured he'd rather say it himself.

"I know," he says, "that the meat stands in high repute and is a Christmastime delicacy but we've been averaging about four a week and I just can't go no more turkey; baked, fried, boiled, hashed nor stewed."

I admit there was a lot in what he said. Mike and me had both been might faithful in this turkey business. After the first few negotiations Iza Belle, which was the turkey woman's name, had said since we were all so well acquainted now there was no use in anybody hiding in the weeds to catch turkeys. Just come one at a time, she said, and she'd bring her wire turkey foot catcher with her and would pick out a nice hen or gobbler herself and give it to us.

But when I told Iza Belle how Jimmy felt about turkey meat she said it was all right not to take one except when we really wanted it, because it was as easy to herd a hundred as ninety-nine.

I went back two days later (the odd days were mine, the even, Mike's) and was sitting in the shade waiting for big Iza when a hard, round something was pushed against my neck. It felt mighty like the front end of a gun.

"Get up and march to the skiff," a voice said.

"Aw golly, Lola," I said, "I'm waiting for somebody."

"March," she said.

I heard the hammer click back cocked.

"For God sakes, Lola," I said, marching, "please hold that thing up in the air and uncock it."

But she wouldn't, and when we got to the boat she made me row down to the island.

She stepped out, still holding that cocked gun on me, and says, "Pull the skiff up in the bushes."

I did.

Next she marched me off to a sandy clearing in the middle of a youpon thicket and tied my feet together and my hands behind me.

You ain't going to shoot me down like a dog, are you, Lola," I said, "and let the buzzards and crows pick my bones? Because God is my witness that I have not done one thing."

"Maybe so," she said, "but your record is fixing to get broke right away."

She leaned the gun against a tree and turned around.

I am sorry that a sense of what is fitting and tellable causes me to omit the next section of this chronicle. You might not believe it anyhow and would think I was slurring the reticence of fair womanhood. I will say this for Lola: she did not really take me there with murder in her heart. Though I do believe she would not have hesitated to shoot me had I refused to do her bidding.

Many times in my life I have had pressure put on me to break my word to friends. I have been tempted by everything from good hot doughnuts to the cold, spilling-over foam of beer in the summertime but never before at the point of a gun.

Would those boys want me to sacrifice my life just in order to keep a promise? Especially one I had made to keep from boxing with Oof? If they would, I decided, they would not be A-No.1 friends anyway. But I knew that they were and would not want me to make the supreme sacrifice. This is about as far as I got with the logic of it because of certain distractions.

After something like an hour I said she might as well untie my hands and feet. I said I wouldn't run off because my promise and good record and just about everything else I held sacred was gone anyway, so she let me loose.

When night came I said maybe we'd better get on back up the river. But she had brought supper in a sirup bucket, and what I mean, I never tasted anything better. Fried pork-shoulder meat in big fat biscuits, and a little bottle of sirup, and a pint jar of boiled black-eyed peas.

I was ashamed of myself to enjoy anything so much that was this sinful but I was nearly starved.

We stayed down on Weenie Island that night and the next day because Lola had brought an extra bucket of groceries. When I finally got back they all said they had been worried to death about me.

I pointed out that they had certainly done it sitting down. Then they wanted to know what happened. I hated to tell. But they kept on hounding me.

Finally I says, "Well, if you must know, you trifling whelps just set here and let me get ravished, that's what."

There was a long silence. I got mad.

"Well, do you censure me or not?" I said.

Jimmy just passed me the bottle.

"Rest easy, little love-weary friend," he said, "little fortunate one, into whose hands the Higher Powers press rubies and pearls and the sky's sweetest nectar. Rest easy and quietly, and do not rob an old friend of a few little secondhand reveries."

Chapter Eleven

Frank had ten acres of sugar cane which by now was ripe. He said if any of us cared to assist at the sirup making he'd appreciate it, and we said we'd be glad to.

That doesn't sound reasonable, I know, but we really were all anxious to help make sirup. Especially after the fine manly way he had forgiven me for getting kidnapped. Frank said he had pretty well guessed what had happened when me and Lola and the gun failed to show up. He said he would have borrowed our skiff and paddled on down to the island that night, except he figured it was too late and since the damage was already done, why not let her go on and get it out of her system.

I said, "Well, I certainly hope you ain't mad at me, Frank."

"Never dreamt of such a thing," Frank said. "You're innocent, Eddie, as a new-born babe, and for me to take out any little grumpiness on you would be mighty cheap indeed."

Of course we all bragged on Frank's broadmindedness and said if more husbands had his kind of sense this would be a far better world to live in.

Right after that was when he brought up the sirup-cooking business, and like I say, we agreed to help.

We had seen the making place many times and I can't tell you why but there was something interesting about it. There was a ten- or fifteen-gallon cooking vat sitting on clay walls about thigh high with a stick-and-mud chimney to carry the smoke away. At a little distance, sitting on a high stump, was the press, or juicer, in which you stuffed stalks of cane. There were two big iron rollers which some cogs turned but what turned the cogs was old Pud or maybe Eagle on the far end of a long oak pole.

We decided to work at night because the gnats were so bad in the daytime that Frank said the sirup would be grainy. Besides, it was moonlight and cooler for working.

Feeding the press was the only job with any real work attached to it, so we let Frank have at it. Mike was supposed to keep the fire going without getting it too hot and burning up the sirup. I said I'd keep Pud moving, and Jimmy said he'd skim.

I guess I need not say that Mike burnt up the first batch with his enthusiasm since Frank had gathered a good pile of wood but the second came off all right and was sirup to make anybody proud. None of your fancy sirup that is just sweet and runny and that's all. This was real old blackstrap with an aftertaste sharp enough to whittle with.

After we'd all said how proud we were of it Frank jugged it and we sopped out the leavings in the vat with some of those big thick Gray Dove biscuits that will ever evoke happy, promise-broke memories in my mind.

But I guess this was all too simple for Mike, who picked some okra in the garden and put it in a fruit jar with some water. Then he screwed the lid on and set it in the vat to cook.

Jimmy said he didn't know Mike liked okra.

"I don't," Mike said, "but with all that good fire it just seems a shame not to cook something more than that eternal sirup."

Then Jimmy composed a song about sirup cooking which hadn't much to it, and we all tried to sing it. But it sounded bad and Jimmy said he guessed we hadn't caught the tune.

We were still trying, though, when Mike's okra jar blew up and sprinkled Pud with hot juice. Which broke up the sirup cooking for that night because Pud ran off with everything but the stump.

Mike said he was sorry and had never known before that there was nitroglycerin in okra. But Frank said it was all right and if he could strain the trash out with some screen wire, maybe the okra would tone down the sirup flavor, which was too strong anyway. Besides, he said, he really hadn't anything important on for tomorrow and might just as well spend it looking for Pud and the sirup mill as not.

We said let us know when he got ready to cook again

and walked down toward camp but before we got there we saw somebody talking to Oof.

Jimmy went on in ahead of us in case it was the constable laying for Mike because of that limbing he gave old Henderson.

But pretty soon Jimmy gave us the come-on signal and when we got there he says, "Boys, shake hands with Johnny Sprix, a traveler by foot, I take it, who struck up with Oof when he saw Oof's fire from the bridge."

We said howdy, Johnny, and have a seat and held out our Durham.

There was some cheese and bread and half a bucket of boiled field peas left over from supper. But hardly had Johnny started in on them before here came a man with one of those peeled willow-switch armchairs that some people tack together and peddle as they go along through the country.

"Hello, boys," he says. "I'm the old willow-chair man. Anybody want to buy a chair?"

"Certainly not," Mike says. "Just plant your back end in it and eat some peas."

"Anything to be agreeable," the chair man said, and sat down and went to eating.

"Now, Johnny," Jimmy said, lighting his pipe, "we were never folks to pry into another man's affairs but we all know the chair man makes chairs and Oof digs wells and the rest of us bridge boys are catchers of fish and cookers of sirup. But we haven't any idea what your business is. We don't want to rush you but the sooner you tell it the quicker we can get comfortable and start talking."

Johnny took the last iron spoonful of peas out of the bucket and ate them and licked the spoon and said, "Well, I'm a Communist."

"That ain't nothing," Mike says. "Jimmy's a Woodman. Or used to be. What's your business?"

"I'm an agitator," Johnny says.

Oof put his oar in here and wanted to know what a Communist was. We explained the best we could that it was somebody that wanted to dynamite the government and don't ask any more questions because all of this was going to be over his head anyhow.

Johnny said the Communists didn't want to blow up the government any more, and Mike said if that was the case the Party had certainly run down from what it used to be.

"Oh, we're not just lazy," Johnny says. "We're trying to bore from within, calmly and gently, until we get enough people seeing it our way. Then we will put the screws on."

He said he guessed we boys were for the Cause.

Jimmy said we like him fine personally but guessed we could struggle along pretty well without any Communism and having old Stalin bossing us around.

"Well, somebody's got to be the boss," Johnny says. "Why not Stalin?"

"Like as not," Jimmy says, "he'd get scared of losing his job and commence purging around and maybe kill a lot of folks."

The trouble with us, Johnny said, was we hadn't any class consciousness and didn't know we were economic slaves. He said the idea of Henry Ford, having that great big car factory in Detroit all to himself, when

121

what right had he to it any more than Jimmy and Mike and me? But Jimmy said old Ford could keep it because it was too big and complicated for Oof to run and he didn't want anything Oof couldn't tend to.

Johnny said he hated to think about it but was afraid we boys were on old Hitler's side.

We told him about the letter and said that was a hell of a thing for him to say when he hadn't more than just licked the last pea off our big spoon.

Then the talk turned to what a hard time the laboring man had and we said yes, wasn't it awful.

He made us a good moving talk on the unions and we promised to go forth and scab no more unless necessity made us, like it did in San Pedro that time. I mean all of us promised besides Oof, who had sat down in the sand and was trying to catch doodlebugs.

Johnny wanted to know if Oof belonged to the union. We said unfortunately he'd never had the opportunity but looked forward to it.

Was Oof's hours long?

For the amount of hole he dug, we said, he worked hardly any hours at all. Besides, in bad weather all he had to do was sit around camp and look pretty.

"I guess," Johnny says, "you don't penalize him for the moods of the weather, which certainly aren't his fault."

This sort of crossed us up. Oof had never got any pay at all, more than his feed and a pair of ducking britches every now and then when the seat of the old ones wore out.

I didn't know what to say and neither did Mike but a twinkle came in Jimmy's eye.

"We will have you know," Jimmy says, "that in fair

weather and foul Oof's emoluments remain exactly the same."

Johnny said good for us and he was glad we had such an advanced view of labor relations. Then he commenced hammering on us again to join the Party.

But Jimmy said if anybody thought we wanted to get regimented into any tractor factory, which seemed to be all they studied about in Russia, or any army, he was full of a certain something.

"What's more," Jimmy says, "we don't want wealth beyond the price of a night's drinking, and no influence whatever, because if I'm any judge, the only people who have any real fun are the nobodies."

Besides, we said, what difference did it make what we believed since nobody was going to pay any attention to us anyhow? We said we were just little private citizens who had trouble enough with the law as it was and no more influence on history than the late W. M. Thackeray, who was a snapping turtle.

Johnny stood up and hitched up his britches and said thanks for the peas and cheese and hospitality but he must be getting on down the road. He said hurrah for our modesty but he would like to leave us with just one little thought he had read out of a book.

We said what was it. And he said every human action committed even by such unimportant little folks as us or the willow-chair man would be like a drop of water falling out of the sky which must land on one side of the Great Divide or the other, and run either to the Atlantic on the right or the Pacific on the left.

Then he went on down the road and left us studying about that.

Finally Mike said Johnny was a dirty Red who had figured around and got us in a spot where everything we did helped either old Hitler or Stalin and he hated both of their guts. He wanted to send Oof after Johnny and have Oof make him take that back about the Great Divide.

But Jimmy said no, it was Mike's fault for blowing hot juice on Pud and making him run away with Frank's mill. Otherwise, he said, we wouldn't have been here to hear it.

Anyway, Mike said, he would pledge allegiance to our flag and fight any Japs that came one inch this side of Catalina Island. But from now on he would do away with the Great Divide in his mind and just imagine everything flat, so when it rained, the water would fall in puddles and not help Hitler or Stalin either one.

Chapter Twelve

T he old willow-chair man hung around several days because there were so many good willow switches growing by the spring and because whenever we ate we set out a plate for him too.

It was about the third night he was there that Mike stepped down to the ditch and in a minute we heard him holler and all remarked, "What on earth do you suppose Mike's got into now?" But the mystery didn't last long because in a minute he skidded into camp saying he was snake-bit and, oh, if a priest was only there to render extreme unction. He was sorry for every sin he'd ever committed and why didn't somebody do something?

We inquired where had he been bit and he told us.

The way Mike was carrying on you'd have thought a bear had bit him. It was plain there would be no peace around there until he got doctored.

The old willow-chair man said he'd always heard warm water would draw out poison. Oof's dishwater was on the fire heating while he took his after-supper nap. I set it off on the ground and we told Mike to sit down in the dishpan.

Well, anybody knows I didn't have a thermometer and certainly could not be expected to see the bubbles rising in there in the dark. And poor Mike was so anxious to get rid of that snake poison that he just flopped down in it and commenced screaming.

Unfortunately, there was not much slope to the sides and the thing lodged on poor Mike with him there yelling bloody murder.

I tried to pull it off and so did Jimmy but it was too hot to do much with. Besides, we couldn't get Mike to hold still.

Finally he made a break for the river and jumped in and I got in there and pulled it off. Then we sent Oof up to Frank's for some axle grease and greased him good.

Of course he got mad at me because the water was too hot but Jimmy wouldn't let him jump on me; so Mike got the lantern and a club and walked bowlegged down to the ditch to take out his bad humor on the snake.

But in a minute he came back holding a sharp forked willow switch in his hand. Then he went up to the chair man and says, "You old son of a bitch, you left this forked stick down there to punch me and make me think it was a snake. Then you talked me into getting fastened up in that bucket of brimstone."

The poor old petrified chair man tried to say he

hadn't done any of it on purpose but he was stammering and Mike wasn't listening.

Mike said certain parts of his own anatomy were probably ruined forever but that was not a circumstance to what he was going to do to the old chair man. But with Oof's help we threw him down and held him while the chair man got to his team and started up the road.

We yelled about this armchair he'd left but all he answered was, "Get up, horses! Run!"

The turkey woman was terribly upset to learn of Mike's disaster and sent him some salve by me which she said would fix the scalded places and at the same time would take care of any little heat rash or eczema that came under its care.

In a day or two Mike could put on his britches and Jimmy collected for a well, so we all decided to go up to the store and have a good canned supper and some beer. But when we got there a lady was standing around waiting for Newt to patch a tire on her Durant touring car.

We stood there a minute tipping our hats. Then Jimmy said he didn't want to intrude but he thought the patch would work better if Newt would tear off the piece of gauze that protected the stickum on the patching.

This made Newt mad but he went ahead and did it, and the lady made a remark about Newt handling that tire like a cub bear trying to thread a needle.

She was tall and pretty and neat built. Her clothes were pretty nice, too, and fit like the label on a bottle.

We said why would careless people leave nails laying

around on the road but she said a nail was not needed to puncture these tires. That they were just contrary enough to blow out with no excuse whatever.

Then she gave us a sort of character sketch of the man who sold the car to her and of his mama, and said in her estimation Mr. Durant hadn't enough mechanical ability to hang a gate.

Jimmy said, oh yes, and wasn't it awful, but her loss was our gain in getting to converse with a handsome lady whose clothes had style and whose language had some flavor to it. Would it be presuming on her good nature to offer to stand her to a cold beer?

She said, no indeed, that Newt had been trying to set 'em up to her but she had refused because she knew nobody got anything in this world for nothing. While she believed in paying her way as she went, she said, there were certain recompenses she didn't care to make to Newt any more than she would to a chimpanzee.

As soon as the ice had been broken she said her name was Daisy and she had lived in a certain part of Galveston with which we were familiar and we might as well switch to whisky.

We were having a good time all right and had Newt open a few cans of tripe and slice some onions. Then some people stopped for gas on their way up to Hackberry to a dance and Daisy said why not take it in.

That suited us fine. If she had said let's go tiger hunting, it would have been just the same.

We sent Oof back to camp.

"Gas up that Durant," Jimmy told Newt, "and water it and oil it and shine up the lights so folks can see us coming."

We got a couple more quarts of whisky and like to had a fight over who would drive but all finally yielded to Mike. Then Mike said the horn wouldn't blow and went in and borrowed Newt's hunting horn.

When he got back I looked out and said Newt's patching job hadn't held.

"I guess the Higher Powers don't want to pamper us after being used to riding in Frank's wagon," Jimmy says. "Just drive on. That old flat tire will come off after about a half a mile and we can proceed unencumbered."

So away we went, never noticing Newt's gas hose was caught in the spare-tire rack and not learning until later we had snatched it out by the roots.

There is no use to follow our progress to Hackberry because I guess the Higher Powers were on the job, and we all got there alive.

Mike and me hadn't any coat and they wouldn't let us in. They said they had passed that rule to keep out the riffraff. We agreed that was reasonable and we didn't want to dance with any riffraff any more than they did, and borrowed coats from the ticket takers, who didn't come under the rule.

It was a really nice affair, attended by, I'm sure, all of Hackberry's upper crust. Nobody was what you would call just dog drunk. Of course, some of the dancers had had a swallow or two like we had but everything went along fine until that constable came up and told Daisy to quit dancing like she was.

"What's wrong with it?" Daisy said.

When he told her she said, "That's the trouble with you blue-law hicks. Not only are you ignorant but you resent anybody else having up-to-date ways."

"Sister," he says, "you'd be surprised how long drunks have been dancing just that way here in Hackberry. Now you either cut out them didoes or get out in the dark to do 'em."

But Daisy wouldn't promise and kept on and finally he caught her by the collar and threw her out.

They squabbled a lot in the door and Daisy said she was coming back in but every time she tried it he caught her and threw her out till she must have plowed up about a half acre of ground with her landing place.

However, the hall was full of other nice girls, and Mike and me was busy trying to find one who would dance with us when all of a sudden we heard a blast from Newt's horn. Both doors of the dance hall burst open and here came Daisy and Jimmy in the Durant.

All the tires were flat and flopping on the wheels. The top had come off and was dragging. Jimmy was standing up blowing Newt's horn and every now and then yelling tallyho.

I tell you it was glorious. Julius Caesar never rode into Rome and made on bit bigger impression on the populace.

It took everybody's breath. The constable just stood there with his mouth open, rubbing his leg where a door timber had hit him. They had almost circled the hall and were ready to drive out when Daisy hollered how did the constable like this. Then everybody commenced whooping and yelling. I guess the constable and me came to about the same time and both realized we had a problem.

There really wasn't time to think so when he started

for the car I just hit him hard in the neck and knocked him down on his face.

Mike had already jumped on the running board and was kicking off ticket takers so I jumped on the other side and told Daisy to gun it.

Maybe the crowd was still kind of mixed up because we went about four hundred yards and drove through a fence into the brush before any cars started. Then we got the whisky and Newt's horn off of the floor and walked on down to the water tower to wait for a train.

I had a wonderful time and Mike did too. We both congratulated Jimmy and Daisy for thinking up something everybody would enjoy so much. They said we did very well when it came to knocking off the ticket takers, and we all agreed there was nothing like a little innocent debauchery to get a person out of a rut.

Anyhow, we were home safe and sound by daylight but all too drunk and footsore for any more frivolity.

We went to sleep.

Next morning my head was killing me. I was afraid to open my eyes for fear they would pop out but I was so water-thirsty I couldn't keep them shut long. For a while, though, I lay there wishing I was laying in the spring with that cool water running over my head and body and down my poor parched throat. Jimmy has often said that those who drink only water never know how good it is, and he is right. I couldn't stand it any longer, and opened my eyes.

When I did, I got a shock, and a bad one.

There lay Miss Daisy just as big as you please in Jimmy's cot and him cuddled up on the ground like a dog, or white trash.

I punched Mike.

At first he couldn't believe his eyes.

Finally he said, "Well, if that don't take the rag off the bush, I don't know what does."

But it wasn't a mistake. When she woke up she went down and jumped in the river to sort of get herself together. Then she came back and with not so much as a kiss-my-foot flopped herself down in Jimmy's willow-switch armchair.

Do you think one of us would have done such a thing? Not on your life.

And did she get so much as a cross word? No. Instead, Jimmy had Oof fork her up the crispest pieces of bacon when we ate and wanted to know if she'd like Oof to flip a little hot grease on the top of her egg so as to done both sides.

We tolerated this kind of thing all day long, watching that Daisy loll on Jimmy's bed and in his chair and getting the best of everything.

That night when the moon came up Jimmy says to her, "Would you care to boat-ride down to our enchanted isle?"

Meaning Weenie.

She said yes, she would.

"Come on, Oof, and row us down there," Jimmy said. "You can have your nap in the skiff while we take a little stroll."

Mike and me sat there just like two clams.

When they were gone Mike went over and sat in the willow-switch armchair.

"Whore," he said.

"I think as much," I said, lying down on the cot.

"Do you suppose," Mike says, "that little bald-head-ed squirt has gone and fell for that strumpet?"

I said I was worried.

Mike suggested some things we might let happen to her accidentally.

I said if Jimmy was crazy about her he'd resent it.

"Well, she's no prettier than Frank's wife," Mike said, "and you gave her up for auld lang syne, didn't you?"

"Yes," I said, "so far as was in my power."

"And what's more," Mike said, "you didn't drag her into camp and give her the only bed and armchair and crisp bacon."

I said it looked like we had been living in Eden and now here come this damned Daisy, snaking around, trying to bust the whole thing up.

But Mike said if he didn't get a drink somewhere he would die anyway, so what was the difference?

We hadn't any money or whisky.

"Let's shoulder that old shotgun," Mike says, "and get the shells and trade them to Newt for a half-dozen good cold beers."

I said Jimmy would be mad but Mike said if we kept the gun he'd kill Daisy and get into trouble and, besides, Jimmy had his mind on a certain something far too much to take any notice of a mere missing shotgun.

We dragged up to the store. When we got there that thieving Newt said, "Only four."

Mike figured a minute and said, "That ain't but forty cents."

Newt said he knew it was but the gun was rusty and had a dirt-dobber nest in the barrel.

133

"Well, what more have you got to do than clean it up?" Mike says. Then he said many ducks would light on the sloughs this winter and doves come to water and quail to pick up spilled maize seeds. "Why, each one of these cartridges," Mike says, "is the same as a good game dinner."

But Newt says, "I guess it would shoot and even throw the empties if you were to soak it in kerosene for a month or two but four bottles is tops."

"Damn you," Mike says, "you know it's worth more than forty cents."

"Maybe so," Newt said, "but you are both nearly dead with hang-overs and dying for a drink, and I know it. So what's the use of giving six when I can get it for four?"

We had to admit he had us but both said we'd die there on the floor before giving him the satisfaction of getting the gun for four lousy beers.

"Well, if you would like to cooperate on a certain matter," Newt says, "I would give you a number of beers free of charge."

We said what was that.

First, he made us promise not to get mad. We said we wouldn't and what did he want.

"Daisy," Newt said.

I saw Mike beginning to grin and kicked him under the counter.

I said, "Newt, I hadn't expected anything decent of you but I didn't think you'd try to frame a poor innocent girl."

Mike caught on reasonably soon and beat on the counter with his fist and called Newt a dirty cad.

I said it was an outrage and Newt's conception of womanhood was no better than a hog's. Hadn't he ever had an old gray-haired mother?

He said we promised not to get mad.

"If you hadn't known you ought to be horse-whipped," I said, "you wouldn't have needed no promise."

Mike said nothing was sacred to Newt beyond getting a profit on groceries.

"All right," Newt says, "I guess I was wrong. Let's just call it off."

Mike grabbed up a chair.

"If you think you can throw poor Daisy aside like a split-fingered glove," Mike yelled, "I'll brain you this minute."

But Newt said if Mike didn't quit acting like a prima donna he wouldn't even discuss the weather with him.

Then Mike said he was as calm as a hen hatching eggs, and we sat down to talk.

When the little matter of emoluments was thrashed out and the main lines of the strategy settled, we had some beers on Newt.

Feeling better, Mike and me eased on back to camp with the shotgun.

About midnight here came the skiff with its cargo of love. Oof said Jimmy told him he was a gondolier and must learn to sing songs in Italian. Mike and me both agreed that was about the most disgusting thing we'd ever heard of.

But we were patient and waited until Jimmy would step down to the ditch or go out to collect for wells. Then we would commence dropping little hints about

Newt, who had money in the bank, and a whisky still, and was fixing to buy a new Essex car.

We would not say anything to Daisy. Just to each other but loud enough for her to hear. Mike told me he was talking to a Mexican lady the other day who had some mighty flattering things to say about Newt personally. He gave it all in detail and said the Mexican lady said she had never really lived before that occasion with Newt.

Then I told him how witty Newt was, and generous, and what a wonderful faith he had in women.

We talked about a lot of women who were trying to get him and finally I said, "Mike, do you suppose our little Daisy would have a chance with Newt?"

Mike laughed.

"Don't be funny," he says. "Newt's too good a catch to mess with any such culls as her."

But whenever Jimmy was there he was treating her like she was Cleopatra, and our river the Nile, and Mike and Oof and me her Nubians.

Then he would go off somewhere and Mike would tell me about the trip Newt was fixing to take to Paris, France, and put up in the best hotel in town. When he got back he was going to have the store painted and a nice cool afternoon gallery nailed onto the east side. When this was all done he would put a line of ladies' silk dresses and drawers and corset covers. Mike said that Newt was still on the fence in regard to handling fur coats.

In the meantime, we had told Oof a hundred times he looked sick. Finally he got where he couldn't eat anything and Jimmy wouldn't let him well-dig and gave him molasses and sulphur against the malaria, which was what Jimmy diagnosed it.

Every now and then Daisy would take a stroll up to the store. The minute she was gone Mike and me would put on a long face and talk about the good old days when we were all real friends and Oof had his health. Then Mike would mention the heroic way I had sacrificed my claim on Frank's wife, Lola.

The grub was getting so low we were all living on boiled vegetables again. The only income we had was from fish, and there weren't any fish because Mike and me wouldn't bait the trap. Of course we let on we baited it but really didn't.

If it had just been a matter of living on boiled okra and squash, which was all the farm afforded right now, I guess Jimmy would have held out a good while. But that spring water was killing him.

It was in our deal with Newt for Mike and me to get a few beers now and then to keep us going but there for eight long, hot, summertime days Jimmy hadn't anything but spring water.

Lots of times he would stand over the spring and cuss it.

"Flow on, foolish fluid," he said one day. "Flow on into the sea and swim sharks and gars and jellyfish. Flow on out of my sight, you diluter of blood, you ruster of guts, you mildewer of good men's souls."

It was cruel, I guess, but we both said we wouldn't torture him like that except to rid him of this vampire, Daisy. Mike said sometimes he had wondered why the Higher Powers had made such a sot of Jimmy but now he saw it was so we could dry him into his senses.

After about the fifth day you could see him wilting by the minute, the royal hue of his nose fading into sort of tired khaki.

Of course Daisy had made certain little remarks about the menu. She said she was born hating squash just like everybody else, and the only good she could see in okra was to use it to grease something with. But Mike and me both knew she would be cutting up a whole lot worse if she hadn't been getting a little snack on the house up at the store every day.

Finally poor Jimmy just had to go to bed. We said what could we get for him. We didn't have what he needed, he said, and if anything happened please bury him on the riverbank with the monument as his tombstone.

Mike and me were both ashamed to look each other in the eye. We felt like dirty dogs that had bit the hand that fed us.

However, we hadn't any intention of wasting all this good suffering we had put poor Jimmy through. We thought the time was about ripe now. But we also knew if it got any riper Jimmy would be dead.

"Jimmy, I hate to even mention it," I said, "and wouldn't if your health hadn't failed you, but that old son of a bitch of a Newt wants Daisy."

"Well, he can't have her," Jimmy said. "Not that she's any good to me right now, but if things get better —"

"Maybe you better not tell him the rest," Mike said. "I know he could withstand the temptation but it would just put him in a worse strain for nothing."

"Go ahead," Jimmy says, "and tell me. I'm not long

for this world anyhow. A few minutes one way or the other won't make much difference."

"Well," I said, "Newt said maybe you wouldn't see it his way but if you cared to let him have Daisy —"

"I will not," Jimmy says.

There was a silence, a pretty long one.

Then he says, "Talk, man. Has the God damned cat got your tongue?"

"All right," I said. "Newt said if you weren't particular about having government stamps on the keg. . . ."

I hesitated because we had banked everything on having tortured him enough, and I just wondered if we had. But I didn't wonder long.

"Don't say any more," Jimmy said to me. "I have heard enough."

Then, before God as my Maker, the color flowed back into his nose and one of the sweetest smiles you ever saw crossed his face. In a minute he sat up and reached for his old shoes. He shook the sand out and put them on. Next he walked over to the grub box and picked up three tin cups but after looking at them a few minutes dropped them in the dirt and took three medium-sized stewpans.

By this time Mike and me were breathing again. Maybe we were jumping at conclusions, but a stewpan in Jimmy's hand can't help but look a lot like a dipper. We both felt like old J. P. Morgan or the King of Sweden because now we were just three old hard-tailed friends again with no damned Daisies in our hair and a keg of whisky waiting for us up the road.

Mike put a tow sack over his shoulder.

"What's that for?" Jimmy says.

139

"To rest the keg on coming home," Mike says.

"Old comrades," Jimmy says, "staunch veterans of a thousand squibbles and squabbles and a few pretty good fist fights, you can put that tow sack down. For though the keg now groaneth with dark brown spirits and would bruise your manly shoulders, the least little frying-size girl could bring it home an hour from now with no harm to her tender flesh."

So Mike put down the sack and we all started up the road wiping the cobwebs out of our stewpans with our shirttails and singing "Beulah Land" with all our might.

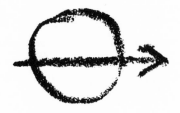

Chapter Thirteen

W hen we got to the store we said, "Where's Daisy?"

"Gone to town to buy a dress," Newt said. "What was it for you boys today?"

"The trade's made," Jimmy said. "I just hope you haven't got far to go for your part of it."

Newt said it was in the back room and wanted Jimmy to sign a paper. But Jimmy said how could Newt expect him to put such a delicate matter in bald legal terms, and just tell Daisy Oof had the bubonic plague and keep away from the bridge.

"Well, I'm not sure but what some of that whisky has leaked out of the keg," Newt said. "The hoops get loose and you can't hardly keep one from leaking."

We said it was perfectly all right with us because his life and not ours would pay for any that was gone.

When he brought it in we thumped it, and it thumped full. Then we filled the stewpans half full of whisky and cut it with about a spoonful of water. I know Jimmy would have liked to christen the keg with a good long toast before we took that first drink but the poor little fellow just couldn't wait. We raised those pans and drank it off.

I think one of the prettiest sights I ever saw was when Jimmy wiped his mouth on his sleeve and said ahhhh. You could see it warming his blood, see peace and contentment flow out in every direction from his stomach, see the lively kindness brimming in his eyes. Most people have never seen the resurrection of a corpse into a fine, living, breathing man. But I saw it, and so did Mike and that unscrupulous Newt.

Right away Jimmy's imagination began to soar.

"It's too bad the Three Musketeers didn't get to know us," he said. "There would have been six men to reckon with — or nine, really, counting D'Artagnan and Frank and Oof.""

Jimmy had told us about those boys a dozen times.

"Wouldn't we have plagued that lousy old Cardinal?" I said.

"We'd have made him wish he'd been born a gal baby," Mike said.

Next we got off on Ponce de León.

Jimmy said he was just a fool, hunting all over Florida for the Fountain of Youth when the first corner saloon would make you twenty years younger for fifty cents. But what kind of friends were we to forget Frank in this hour of triumph?

We said let's go get him.

It was cloudy and fixing to rain. Already it was sprinkling. Mike said Jimmy would catch cold.

"As long as a man can keep the clouds out of his soul, what difference does it make?" Jimmy said. "Besides, that first panful has made me twice as waterproof as a duck."

Also, Daisy would show up pretty soon, and might make remarks about the trade. And Mike and me was anxious to get on back to camp and tell Oof he looked well again. We certainly didn't want him to die and have everybody saying we conjured him.

In no time at all we were back in camp and had Oof well and Frank drunk. We just sat there perfectly happy listening to the rain drumming on the bridge and watching it frost the river.

Then mighty calm and patiently, with all the time in the world before him, Jimmy reasoned out why it was best and honorable to swap Daisy off for this keg of better than average whisky.

He said he guessed the Higher Powers had meant us to live like wild free studhorses roaming the face of the earth and gladdening whatever hearts we run across.

Mike said suppose a brick fell off the bridge and cold-cocked one of us, especially Jimmy, and we had to bury him here beside the river and plod our lonely little two-thirds way down life's road.

I tried to stop him but his mind had already set on it. He was crying now and said what would we do when night came in strange far-off places, our hearts eaten out by glorious memories, and us just two old unloved and probably sick-sober wayfarers?

I said I guessed I could stand the sober part but could never lift a whisky glass without my poor heart being wrung by thoughts of the high comradeship we had known in a hundred jails and saloons and boot-legging joints.

What would hurt him most, Mike said, was the sound of a player piano, wafting back recollections of gaiety and romance and friendly tiffs in just about every whorehouse between Key West and Tacoma.

From this we went to what a disappointment we had all been to our folks. We were far too mean to go to school, much less study or leave the poor teacher alone.

About midnight the river commenced rising and we had Oof move everything as high as he could get it from the water. And by noon the next day, rain or no rain, we had to get up on top of the bridge with our stuff.

That rain was mighty cold but we had only drunk a couple of gallons of whisky and had plenty left against any reasonable inclemency. However, when the water began running over the ends of the bridge, that was something else again.

It had long since spread all over the Bottoms and washed poor Frank's crops away but Frank said he was never one to complain: if it just left the farm, he'd have other years to try it in.

"What about Lola?" I said.

"Oh, I guess she'll rustle around and make out someway," Frank said. "More than likely she'll come riding down this way as soon as the old house floats off the blocks."

In about an hour then, sure enough, here she came riding on the roof and we all got ready to catch her as the house busted against the bridge. When we did, she said she hated to break in on our little stag party and wouldn't except she hadn't had any rudder on the house.

Her clothes were damp, so I mixed her a little toddy, thinking how nice it would be if only Lola and me were marooned on this bridge and she had a machine gun and some handcuffs and two or three of those sirup buckets full of dinner.

"I could get the least bit drunker," Jimmy says, "which I'd like to do in case I have to meet my Maker and try to explain a few things, but if I did I'd fall off the bridge sure as the world."

Anyhow we all talked about what we'd say in case we met Him and helped each other think up excuses. We all said we'd say whatever we had done had been an error of the head and not the heart. Nobody was to breathe a word about Mike whipping old man Henderson, or mine and Lola's little trip to the island. But Frank said go ahead and tell Him.

"If I'm man enough to forgive you dern brats," Frank says, "He certainly ought to could. After all, Lola ain't no wife of His'n."

I said, "Thanks, Frank. That touches my heart. But we can't tell how He'll take it. I'm in an awful spot to say it but I figure if He had your sense He'd handle His rain better."

Jimmy said please lay off the Higher Powers.

"I think as much," Mike says, "at least till this damned river goes down."

But finally we got tired of waiting, not having slept in two nights, and went to sleep.

Next day somebody punching me woke me up.

"What's the matter?" I said, and rubbed my eyes.

But nobody said anything so I looked around.

Then I saw it. The sky was clear and the river was falling. But our camping end of the bridge was gone.

I felt queer and didn't say anything either.

At last Jimmy says, "Well, they've spoke and I reckon there can't be any doubt about what they mean."

We said we guessed not and all just stood there, sobered and sad.

On the following day we found out Newt had drowned. Mike and me was tickled to death but Jimmy was furious. He said he had spent days working on Sam's case of foul play and had the proof all worked out on Newt and now it was wasted.

Anyhow we went up there and buried the old hellion and nailed up the store door. I don't know what became of Daisy and certainly don't care.

We meant to go in business as soon as the stock dried out but the very next day a man gave Jimmy fifteen hundred dollars to sign a quitclaim for his damages from the railroad for killing poor Sam.

That was more money than we could have made anyway as merchants, what with our appetites, so we gave Frank and Lola legal title to the store.

Of course this money like to have bothered the life out of us. We hadn't any way to spend fifteen hundred dollars, though we knew somebody would steal it or we would lose it out of our pockets if we didn't.

Finally Mike said, "Let's get on the train and go to Houston. We'll put up in the best hotel they've got and have high-priced stuff charged till we get rid of that cussed money."

That sounded good.

146

"What about our pals?" I said.

"Well, I hope to God you didn't think I meant to leave them here," Mike says.

Then I said, "What about Oof? They won't let colored folks stay in these Southern hotels."

This worried us but in the end Jimmy figured it out. He said we'd wrap up Oof's head in a towel and make him some long-crotched britches out of a bed sheet. We'd call him the Rajah Oof del Krim of India and would be his retinue.

"That way," he says, "those hotel people will not know how to be nice enough to any of us."

So we invited Frank and Lola and the turkey woman and they were all tickled to death to come.

When we got ready to go the turkey woman had made a bushel basket full of lunch, and poor Oof looked an awful silly sight. Frank was sweating under two forty-eight pound sacks of Gray Dove. We tried to get him to leave them but he said the hotel might not have any and he didn't want to be having one headache right after another on his trip.

As we stopped to take a last look at this place where we had known so much friendship and happiness, we all expected Jimmy to say something that would give our hearts a twist and leave us with the bittersweet flavor of sadness in our mouths.

But he didn't say a word. He just stooped and picked up one of those old red Brazos Bottom clods and touched it to his lips. Then he crumbled it and let it blow away in the breeze. I guess a few grains landed in the two big tears running down his face.

Nobody said anything.

Then he turned around and we followed him down the road.

The chapter that follows was written by Perry for a second edition but was never published. The original handwritten manuscript and an accompanying typescript are in the Perry Collection at the Harry Ransom Humanities Research Center at the University of Texas at Austin. It is used with their permission.

Chapter Fourteen

I think this was Saturday morning and we were all just sitting there listening to Mike tell about a girl he used to know named Lena. He was telling us a lot about Lena's little ways and what she liked and was capable at when we looked up and saw this building coming down the river. There was about a three- or four-foot rise on that must have been caused by one of the little rivers that runs into the Brazos getting on a rampage. Anyway just as soon as we saw it coming around the bend we knew what it was. Most of the steeple had been knocked off where it had floated under bridges but the rest of it was in first class shape outside of maybe needing a few coats of paint.

As it came on down we just sat there. I guess we were scared. When it got about a hundred yards from Weenie Island we commenced to holding our breath.

First an eddy carried it towards the right hand channel, then a cross current caught it and switched it to the left. But it didn't stay there. It circled and floated smack dab up on the end of the island.

I looked at Mike.

He never said anything. But he nodded at me.

Jimmy didn't even look up. He just sat there staring into the open front doors which were aimed straight at us.

Finally Jimmy said, "Maybe the river will rise some more and it will float away."

But it didn't.

I guess we sat there for an hour waiting for Jimmy to say something.

Finally Mike looked at me and said, "I've heard of folks being out plowing and saw God in the clouds but this is the first time I ever heard of a good clapboard church being furnished with the call."

I said it was a miracle.

"If I was smart," Mike said, "or a good talker I wouldn't hesitate for a minute. It just so happens that I ain't."

"Me neither."

We waited some more.

Finally Jimmy stood up and said, "All right. Since I got eyes to see, so may it be. Pass the word around."

"What time?" I said.

"Eleven o'clock," Jimmy said, mighty sober. "That's regulation. Since there ain't any kids around, we won't need to hold Sunday School."

That's all he said. He walked off up the bank.

I guess you don't need to be told that everybody sat up and took notice when they heard Jimmy was going to preach on Sunday at the Weenie Island Church. Everybody cleaned up and put on their best Sunday morning and bailed out their skiffs. Frank and Lola were there, and Newt, and Isa Belle, the turkey woman, and Stripes and Aleck, and Mexican Pete and his outfit. Naturally all of us bridge boys was there. Even old man Henderson showed up. He sat on a back pew and held his knife open but he was there just the same.

As the time drew near everybody got quiet and Jimmy walked up to the pulpit.

"Folks," he said, "this ain't my fault. We was just sitting on the river bank listening to Mike when here comes this church down the channel and lodged on the island. You've seen those posters wanting you to join the army where Uncle Sam points his finger at you. Well the powers above took aim on me in just that way with these church doors.

"Now I may be scabbing, preaching here without a card, and furthermore there ain't a Bible, looks like, this side of Hackberry, but I been drafted so I'll just have to do my best."

We all clapped and Jimmy said thanks.

"If I had a Bible here," he said, "I could read you what you ought to do. You wouldn't understand it, nor me either, but we would know it was O.K. But since we haven't got one, I'll just have to make up as I go along.

"And just to make a long story short, if everybody would do right, and maybe get together and beat hell out of everybody that didn't, we would make out very well.

"Of course most of us is a little short on understanding other folkses' ways but we're also a little short on trying.

"I know none of us is perfect. Even me and Mike and Eddie might err a little now and then in the direction of drinking too much whiskey. At least we don't mean no harm.

"But it's something else again to go around sitting folks on railroad tracks and profiteering on groceries."

We all clapped and whistled and stomped.

"The trouble is," Jimmy says, "that while there are a lot of friendly, pure-hearted folks in this world there is also a lot which I can only denominate by the unecclesiastical term: sons of bitches.

"Spose we were all just fair. Not really swell guys, or real generous but just downright fair whether we owned a factory or worked in one. Spose we all really believed other folks didn't like to suffer, and just because we were smart, didn't deserve anymore than enough. The hell of it is when two other folks are mixed in a deal we believe they ought to be fair. But when it's us, business is business.

"But the main trouble is us simple folks don't know what's going on these days. In the time of the Ark when all the plain folks was drowning, they drowned just the same but they knew what was the matter. Too much water. We're not even sure we know what's wrong. Maybe you do. I don't"

We all said we didn't either.

"We just know we live in a world where Hitler is bad and old Mussolini, and the devil, and probably Stalin and Roosevelt and the Liberty League. And I don't like it any more than you.

"Our real enemies is boll weevils and blow- outs and leaky skiffs and the mumps. It ain't too smart to say

152

that because everybody knows it, but why are we so God damned helpless we can't do nothing but fight one another and get nowhere?"

Of course nobody with any sense would have tried to answer that. There was a might big silence.

Oof stood up.

"Man children smarter than dog children," Oof said. "They know more bad tricks. Takes longer get grown. But they get there. One day they all get grown and say, 'We all brothers. All friends.' Funny, huh? We all row boat same way. We get there. We finally learn right song to pull by."

Mike jerked Oof down in his seat and said, "Everybody please excuse Oof who is a poor heathen but don't mean no harm."

"Shut up, Mike," Jimmy said. "Oof had said what I been trying to. Well that's what we need. That the biggest, most important questions that lies hidden somewhere out in the dark. What is that new song? Maybe there's some old one everybody's forgot. Maybe none of it has ever been heard before. But that's what all good men ought to be looking for now. That's our Holy Grail. That new song that everybody can sing to. . . ."

Right here Isa Belle commenced screaming and says, "Break for the skiffs cause the river had rose and the church is floating off!"

Well everybody run and, I'm thankful to say, made it.

Back on shore after the church had gone on out of sight down the river, everybody said they had enjoyed the sermon fine except Frank was disappointed because it broke up before he could be saved again. He said it

153

always gave him such a good clean airy feeling to be able to join the church at the end of the meeting, but since he'd already joined twenty-seven times, guessed he could make out on that.

Then Jimmy asked Oof how come him to say what he did, but Oof said he didn't know and was just glad it seemed to make sense.

We went on home.